P9-DTB-663

AP

TAG-ALONG BETH

Beth's older sister, Brittany, turned to Julie. "Didn't I hear that there was tiny tot skiing here at Stony Lookout? Beth could be part of that!"

Brian laughed. Beth felt her cheeks flush.

"Come on, Brittany," said Julie. "Don't give your sister such a hard time. She's the right age for the beginners' lessons. Anybody over six can take them."

Brittany threw back her head and laughed uproariously, as if Julie's comment were the funniest thing she'd ever heard.

"Is this what's known as sibling rivalry?" Julie asked. "I'm an only child so I wouldn't know."

An only child! thought Beth. *How lucky can you get!*

Bantam Skylark Books by Betsy Haynes
Ask your bookseller for the books you have missed

THE AGAINST TAFFY SINCLAIR CLUB
TAFFY SINCLAIR STRIKES AGAIN
TAFFY SINCLAIR, QUEEN OF THE SOAPS
TAFFY SINCLAIR AND THE ROMANCE MACHINE DISASTER
BLACKMAILED BY TAFFY SINCLAIR
TAFFY SINCLAIR, BABY ASHLEY, AND ME
TAFFY SINCLAIR AND THE SECRET ADMIRER EPIDEMIC
TAFFY SINCLAIR AND THE MELANIE MAKE-OVER
THE TRUTH ABOUT TAFFY SINCLAIR
TAFFY SINCLAIR GOES TO HOLLYWOOD
NOBODY LIKES TAFFY SINCLAIR
THE GREAT MOM SWAP
THE GREAT BOYFRIEND TRAP

Books in The Fabulous Five series
1 SEVENTH-GRADE RUMORS
2 THE TROUBLE WITH FLIRTING
3 THE POPULARITY TRAP
4 HER HONOR, KATIE SHANNON
5 THE BRAGGING WAR
6 THE PARENT GAME
7 THE KISSING DISASTER
8 THE RUNAWAY CRISIS
9 THE BOYFRIEND DILEMMA
#10 PLAYING THE PART
#11 HIT AND RUN
#12 KATIE'S DATING TIPS
#13 THE CHRISTMAS COUNTDOWN
#14 SEVENTH-GRADE MENACE
#15 MELANIE'S IDENTITY CRISIS
#16 THE HOT-LINE EMERGENCY
#17 CELEBRITY AUCTION
#18 TEEN TAXI
#19 THE BOYS-ONLY CLUB
#20 THE WITCHES OF WAKEMAN
#21 JANA TO THE RESCUE
#22 MELANIE'S VALENTINE
#23 MALL MANIA
#24 THE GREAT TV TURNOFF
#25 THE FABULOUS FIVE MINUS ONE
#26 LAURA'S SECRET
#27 THE SCAPEGOAT
#28 BREAKING UP
#29 MELANIE EDWARDS, SUPER KISSER
#30 SIBLING RIVALRY

Super Editions
#1 THE FABULOUS FIVE IN TROUBLE
#2 CARIBBEAN ADVENTURE
#3 MISSING YOU

THE FABULOUS FIVE

Sibling Rivalry

BETSY HAYNES

A BANTAM SKYLARK BOOK®
NEW YORK • TORONTO • LONDON • SYDNEY • AUCKLAND

RL 5, 009–012

SIBLING RIVALRY
A Bantam Skylark Book / March 1992

ISBN 0-553-15875-9

Published simultaneously in the United States and Canada

Bantam Books are published by Bantam Books, a division of Bantam Double-
day Dell Publishing Group, Inc. Its trademark, consisting of the words
"Bantam Books" and the portrayal of a rooster, is Registered in U.S. Patent
and Trademark Office and in other countries. Marca Registrada. Bantam
Books, 666 Fifth Avenue, New York, New York 10103.

PRINTED IN THE UNITED STATES OF AMERICA

OPM   0 9 8 7 6 5 4 3 2 1

CHAPTER

1

*B*eth Barry slumped back against the middle seat in her family's station wagon and rested her cheek against the cool windowpane. As she glanced absently at the snow-covered countryside rushing by, she tried to tune out the babble of happy conversation swirling around her in the crowded car. She wished she could be as excited as the rest of her family about spending their winter vacation skiing at Stony Lookout Resort. But the truth was, she was miserable. She closed her eyes, remembering the scene at the dinner table when her parents had broken the news.

"But, Mom! Dad! We can't possibly go away *then*!" she'd cried, letting her fork drop and clatter

1

into her plate. "That's Winter Carnival! Remember? The whole town will be there, and they have snow sculpture contests, and a tug-of-war between kids from Wakeman Junior High and the high school. And then there's the Ice Skaters' Ball on the last night, when everybody dances on skates at the rink in the park and they crown the Snow Prince and Princess. We can't *possibly* miss *that*! My friends and I have been planning to go for weeks!"

"Personally, I can't wait to go skiing," Brittany, her sixteen-year-old sister, had said dryly. "There are bound to be tons of gorgeous guys at Stony Lookout. Besides, don't worry, little sis. You aren't going to be crowned Snow Princess at the Winter Carnival, anyway."

Mr. Barry had put his coffee cup down slowly and looked at Beth. "Sweetheart, of course we know it's Winter Carnival," he had said patiently. "And Winter Carnival is certainly a big event around here. But a ski vacation is special. Remember how you've always said you wanted to learn to ski? Well, now's your chance."

From the chair beside her, Beth's twelve-year-old brother Todd had piped up, "Wow! This is going to be the best vacation we've ever had. I can't wait to get my skis on, and wait'll you see me streaking down those slopes! VROOOOM!" He had plunged his left arm down an imaginary slope, stopping his hand an instant before it could crash into Beth's plate. Then he'd given her a devilish grin.

Beth had scowled back, thinking how immature twelve-year-old boys could be. "You'll probably break your neck," she had muttered.

"Here, look at the brochure," her mother had said, handing it across the table to Beth.

"Let me see, too," six-year-old Alicia had cried, jumping off her chair and crowding in between Beth and Todd for a closer look. "Can Agafa come, too?"

Her father had chuckled. "I'm afraid there are no dogs allowed, Alicia. We'll have to leave Agatha here in the kennel."

"I could stay home and take care of her," Beth had offered hopefully, even though she knew how her parents would respond.

"Don't be silly, Beth," her mother had replied. "You know we would never allow you to stay home alone."

"But the rest of The Fabulous Five could stay with me," she had pleaded.

"Will you please just look at the brochure?" her mother had asked with a trace of irritation.

Beth had sighed and glanced at the pamphlet. It was full of photographs of both adults and good-looking teenagers in bright ski outfits standing in groups on the ski slopes, swimming in the indoor swimming pool, and having dinner in a quaint, rustic dining room. One especially beautiful picture had caught her eye. It showed skiers coming down a slope at night holding bright lanterns.

But it isn't Winter Carnival, she had thought miserably. And none of my friends will be there. They'll all be here, having the time of their lives *without me*.

"It says in the brochure that they have dances at night, too. I'll bet Brian and I will really enjoy those," Brittany had added, giving Beth a superior look. "They aren't for *kids*, you know."

Beth had blinked in anger. "I'm not a kid, Brittany! I can do anything you can do."

"Yeah, right." Brittany had smirked and nudged seventeen-year-old Brian, who sat beside her.

Beth had been furious at Brittany. Her older sister always called her a little kid and treated her that way, too. It wasn't fair. After all, Beth was only three years younger than Brittany. Occasionally Mrs. Barry tried to console Beth when Brittany was particularly nasty, saying that it was just normal sibling rivalry and Beth shouldn't let it get to her. Well, normal or not, I'd love to show Brittany just how wrong she is, Beth thought angrily, but *not* if it means missing Winter Carnival and having fun with my friends.

Now, as her father turned onto an asphalt road, Beth forgot her anger and sucked in her breath at the sight of the beauty all around her. Flanking the road were tall pine and white paper birch trees, and in the western sky the sun was dipping toward a pink-and-blue frosted mountain. Beth wished the other members of The Fabulous Five had been able to come along with her to see the spectacular view of the mountains. The five of them—Jana Morgan, Christie Winchell, Melanie Edwards, Katie Shannon, and Beth—had been best friends for as long as Beth could remember. They had done everything together, until recently, when Christie had moved with her family to London. The rest of The Fabulous Five missed her terribly, and now were planning to visit her in England over spring break. They were all saving every penny they could to help cover expenses.

"I believe we've arrived," Mr. Barry suddenly announced.

They had just pulled out of the woods, and the resort came into view. A large, two-story wooden building drew Beth's attention first.

"It's huge," said Todd.

Mrs. Barry nodded. "It used to be a dairy barn. See the two wings on either end of the building?"

The kids murmured yes.

"The cows were kept there, in stalls. That's where the guest rooms are."

Todd leaned forward and yanked on a strand of Beth's short hair. "Moooo! Beth will fit right in."

"Todd, you're incredibly immature," Beth answered. "Mom, tell him to shut up."

"Kids," Mrs. Barry warned, "we want this to be a very pleasant vacation, so please try to get along."

Mr. Barry pulled the car up next to the lodge. "Everybody stay put while I register. Then we'll go to our rooms and unpack."

Beth waited impatiently while her father was gone. She watched several young people go by, hoping to spot someone close to her age. She didn't see anyone who fit into that category, but there sure seemed to be a lot of little kids about Alicia's age running around. This definitely was a family place.

Mr. Barry returned a few minutes later. He drove slowly around the lodge to one wing and parked next to the entrance in the middle. "Everybody take a suitcase," he ordered.

The family piled out of the station wagon, everyone hauling out a piece of luggage, and followed Mr. Barry inside and up the stairs. He led them to the end of the hall and unlocked one of the doors. When the door swung open, Beth could see that the room was paneled in yellow knotty pine and decorated in blue. There were two double beds.

"Brian and Todd, you take this one," said their father.

The boys nodded and shoved their suitcases into the room.

"This will be your room, girls," said Mrs. Barry, opening a second door. "Beth, you share the far bed with Alicia, and Brittany can take the other bed."

"But Alicia thrashes in her sleep!" Beth protested. "She kicks me every time I sleep in the same bed with her."

"I don't mean to kick you, Bethy," Alicia told her.

"Of course you don't, honey," her mother said.

"I didn't mean she was trying to hurt me," Beth insisted. "But I have a hard time sleeping when she socks me in the face and kicks my legs all night."

"You'll survive," Mrs. Barry assured her.

"Just this once, couldn't Brittany sleep with Alicia?" Beth pleaded.

"We'll hear no more about it," Mrs. Barry said, and left to go to her room across the hall. "Beth, help Alicia unpack, will you?"

Brittany smiled triumphantly at Beth. "Just one of the advantages of being older," she commented airily.

Beth let out a sigh of exasperation and angrily threw her suitcase and Alicia's little travel bag on her bed and opened them. It just isn't fair, she thought. Brian and Brittany get all the privileges, Alicia gets babied all the time, and Todd's too busy playing Nintendo or shooting baskets with his friends to care. And what am I? Just stuck in the middle! No privileges. No attention. Nothing.

"I'll take the top two bureau drawers," Brittany announced, "and you and Alicia can have the bottom two."

"Why should you get an extra drawer?" Beth demanded.

"Because, dear little sister," Brittany replied, as if she were talking to a five-year-old, "I brought more clothes than you did. Besides, I don't want to crush my things."

"Well, I don't want *my* things crushed, either," said Beth. "We'll share the second drawer."

"No way," said Brittany.

Beth watched Brittany unpack, her blood boiling. If Brittany got the bed all to herself, there was no way she was going to get an extra drawer, that was for sure!

Beth unpacked, then helped Alicia put her things in the bottom drawer, watching Brittany out of the corner of her eye the whole time. Beth hung her clothes in the closet and stuffed the rest into the one bureau drawer.

"Finished!" Brittany said after a few minutes as she headed out the door. "See you later!"

As soon as the door closed behind Brittany, Beth stormed over to the bureau, pulled open the second drawer, shoved Brittany's carefully laid-out clothes to one side, and put some of her own things in the space she'd made.

"There!" She smiled to herself. "Now *I'm* finished!"

"Me, too," added Alicia.

"Come on," Beth said, closing the door and leading her little sister across the hall to her parents' room. Todd was sitting in the middle of their bed playing his portable Nintendo. "Where are Brian and Brittany?" Beth asked.

"Oh, they went to look for something to do," said her mother as she hung up her ski jacket.

"Already? Why didn't they wait?" moaned Beth. "I want to see the place, too!"

"Go ahead and explore with Todd and Alicia," suggested her mother.

I'm with the little kids again! Beth fumed. *It's not fair! I'm as mature as Brian and Brittany, but I always get stuck with the babies!*

She turned to her younger brother and sister. "Well, come on," she said crossly. "Let's go."

This vacation has got to get better, Beth thought as they left their parents' room and started down the hall. It couldn't possibly get any worse!

CHAPTER

2

*B*eth stomped downstairs ahead of Todd and Alicia.

Midway down, Alicia stopped and tugged at Beth's sweater. "Bethy, I want to know something."

Beth sighed. "What?"

"Well, in the pictures sometimes the swimming pool was outside and sometimes it was inside. Same with the tennis courts. How come?"

Beth smiled in spite of herself. She started to answer, but Todd interrupted.

"See, they're both outside in the summertime. Then what they do in the winter is they roll up the tennis court like a rug and haul it inside. Then they lift the swimming pool out of the ground and plug it

11

into a hole they've made especially for it inside," he said, grinning.

"Todd." Beth shook her head. "Todd's teasing you, Alicia. But they do something almost as amazing. In the winter the swimming pool and tennis courts are covered with huge plastic bubbles that are filled with warm air. That way you can be warm inside while you swim and still be able to see the snow and mountains all around you."

"Wow," said Alicia, her voice filled with wonder. "Let's go find them. I want to see the bubbles."

"We'll see them in a little while," Beth assured her.

Alicia's childish question had perked up Beth's spirits a little, and she started down the steps again with Todd and Alicia following. When they reached the bottom, Todd pointed down a long hallway and said, "I bet the lodge is that way."

He was right. They pushed open a glass door at the end of the hall and found themselves in the great room of the lodge. There was a roaring fire in the huge stone fireplace, and small clusters of sofas and chairs were arranged around the room. Old-fashioned lanterns hanging overhead created a soft glow.

"Neat," exclaimed Todd.

"Yeah," agreed Beth, looking around the room. A man and woman with a little boy about Alicia's age had just come in the front door and were stomping snow off their boots. Their faces were red from the cold, and the little boy was grinning from ear to ear as he hurried toward the fireplace to warm. Beth felt an instant twinge of envy. Maybe by this time tomorrow she, too, would be skiing. She would never admit it to her parents, of course, but the idea of skiing was exciting.

"Hey, look over there," shouted Todd. He was pointing toward Brian and Brittany, who were across the room talking to three teenage girls. Two of the girls were blond, and the third had reddish brown hair. They were all drinking hot chocolate and chattering away.

"It figures," Beth muttered under her breath. Naturally, Brian and Brittany would find kids their own ages right away. They didn't have to baby-sit Todd and Alicia.

She edged away from Todd and Alicia and moved closer to the older kids, trying to hear what the girls were saying.

"This room is where all the skiers come to warm up after a day on the slopes," one of the girls said, twirling a fat marshmallow floating at the top of her cup. "And the fire is kept going twenty-four hours a day."

"Wow," said Brittany. "That sounds romantic."

The three girls and Brittany giggled.

"That's not all," a second girl added. "A band plays every evening, and they're terrific. Then on Saturdays there's night skiing, when everyone comes down the mountain carrying lanterns." She smiled at Brian. "You're going to love it here."

"Gosh, it sure sounds like it," he replied.

"What a flirt," Beth murmured to herself, as she watched Brian return the girl's smile.

"By the way," said one of the blond girls, "I'm Julie, that's Sarah"—she pointed to the other girl who was blond—"and that's Molly. The three of us met four years ago when our families were here at the same time. We've come back every year, and this year we were allowed to come by ourselves."

"We're having a *blast*!" said Molly, brushing a strand of reddish-brown hair out of her eyes and looking straight at Brian.

Beth listened enviously. Imagine coming here with a group of friends, *without having your family around*! She could picture The Fabulous Five schussing down the slopes together, sitting around the fire drinking hot chocolate, and then dancing the night away with handsome skiers. It sounded like heaven.

"Do you all ski?" asked Brittany, bringing Beth back to the present.

"A little," Sarah answered. "We're certainly not experts, though."

"Do you ski, Brian?" asked Molly.

Brian shook his head. "No, but I want to learn."

"Me, too," said Brittany. "We're going to have to take lessons."

"Hey, join us," the girls said in chorus.

"First thing in the morning," Julie told them. "We'll all go to the beginners' class together."

Brittany looked doubtful. "Are you sure? I thought you were all skiers."

"Uh, we could use some more pointers," Sarah replied, and the other two grinned at her knowingly. Beth wondered what that was all about.

"Great," said Brittany.

Just then the door to the outside opened again, and a group of kids about Beth's age stomped inside, bringing a blast of cold air in with them. Beth searched their faces for a potential friend. Her heart sank. All of them were boys, and not one looked the least bit interesting. They all had snow packed onto their pants, wild, windblown hair, and red cheeks and noses. They were talking in loud, enthusiastic voices about their skiing feats of the day.

"Hotdoggers," Julie commented, waving her hand dismissively.

"Excuse me?" asked Brian.

"Hot-dog skiers," Julie said. "You know, always trying crazy stunts on the slopes. You can spot them because their skis are always longer than everyone else's, and they've got that kamikaze look in their eyes. You'll usually find them coming down The Jaws of Death."

"What's that?" asked Brittany.

"It's the toughest slope here," Julie replied. "Only people who are *insane* go down it."

Out of the corner of her eye Beth saw Todd's eyebrows shoot up, and an instant later he was eagerly approaching the boys. Alicia followed him, staring at the boys in open-mouthed fascination. Todd ignored her as he began talking with the skiers.

Beth was left standing alone. She glanced toward Todd and Alicia. Their attention was fixed upon the hot-dog skiers, and they had forgotten she was there. Next she looked in the direction of the teenagers. Maybe she could hang around with them for a while, at least until she found someone her own age.

"Why not?" she whispered. It might be a good chance to prove to Brittany that she wasn't just a little kid. Actually, this looked like the perfect opportunity to join in. Beth hurried to the hot chocolate dispenser and filled a cup, then casually sauntered over to the group and stood next to Brittany.

At first it seemed as if her sister didn't notice her. But then she heard Brittany whisper harshly, "What do *you* want?"

Beth was determined to stay cool. "I'm having hot chocolate. Do you mind?"

Brittany rolled her eyes toward the ceiling and then turned back to the group.

"So what time do the lessons begin in the morning?" Beth blurted out.

Brittany gave Beth a look that was absolutely meant to kill. "Butt out, Beth," she growled. "Go find someone your own age to play with."

"Is this your sister?" asked Julie.

Brittany nodded, but she didn't speak.

Beth felt a tight ball of anger form inside her chest. Brittany is hoping that if she ignores me, I'll go away, she thought.

"Hi," Julie greeted Beth. Molly and Sarah smiled and chimed in their hellos, too.

Beth forced a smile. "Hi, I'm Beth." Suddenly she wanted badly to be one of them. They were obviously having such a good time, and there wasn't *that* much difference in their ages. "I'm really eager to learn to ski," she added hopefully.

Brittany turned to Julie. "Didn't I hear that there was tiny tot skiing here at Stony Lookout? Beth could be part of that!"

Brian laughed. Beth felt her cheeks flush.

"Come on, Brittany," said Julie. "Don't give your sister such a hard time. She's the right age for the beginners' lessons. Anybody over six can take them."

Brittany threw back her head and laughed uproariously, as if Julie's comment were the funniest thing she'd ever heard. Then Brittany snapped her fingers. "Oh, well, Beth. It's too bad, but you're just over the age limit for tiny tots."

Beth's blood was boiling, but she forced herself to keep her mouth shut. She didn't dare let her temper get out of control and make a fool out of her.

"You sure have a big family," Molly remarked.

"We sure do," Brittany agreed with a definite lack of enthusiasm.

"There are five kids in the family," said Beth.

Brittany made a face. "I'm sure Molly can count, Beth."

The girls laughed, and Julie looked at Molly. "Is this what's known as sibling rivalry?" When Molly laughed and nodded, Julie added, "I'm an only child, so I wouldn't know."

An only child! Beth thought. *How lucky can you get!*

"How lucky can you get!" Brittany said, echoing Beth's thoughts. "I can't imagine what it would be like not to have little kids under foot all the time."

Everyone looked at Beth and laughed again.

Beth smiled back through clenched teeth. Keep your chin up, she told herself. Show them you're as mature as they are.

Luckily her parents entered the great room just then and approached them.

"Hi," Mrs. Barry said, glancing at the three girls sitting with Brittany, Brian, and Beth.

"Hi, Mom and Dad," replied Brittany. She introduced the girls to her parents.

"It's nice to meet you," said Mrs. Barry, and Mr. Barry smiled and nodded. "But it's time for dinner so we'll have to pull Brian, Brittany, and Beth away for a while."

"Great. I'm famished," said Brittany. "Brian and I will see you guys later."

And me, too! Beth thought, but she knew better than to say it out loud.

CHAPTER

3

*B*eth glanced around the dining room as she followed her parents to a table. It was a big room, paneled in knotty pine, like the rest of the resort. There was a large dance floor in the front of the room, and all the tables were covered with red-and-white checkered tablecloths. Small red candles sat in the center.

The Barrys chose a table by a window that looked out at the mountain. The last skiers of the day were gracefully drifting down the snow-packed slopes toward the lodge. Beth sighed, trying to imagine how it would feel to be one of them.

When the family was seated, a waitress came to their table and filled their water glasses. "I'm

Cindy," she said. "For dinner you have your choice of steak or chicken. I'll bring the vegetables in bowls, and if you need more of anything, all you have to do is holler."

Cindy brought them bowls heaped with mashed potatoes, gravy, corn, and green beans. Then she brought a cutting board with a loaf of bread and a knife, and gave them plates with the entrees they had ordered.

While the rest of the family talked and laughed, Beth picked at her food and stared out the window. All the skiers had left the slopes, but that hardly mattered. She was still smarting from Brittany's nasty comments in front of the three girls in the great room. Why did Brittany always treat her like a baby?

Well, maybe it's a good thing there aren't any girls my age here at Stony Lookout, she thought, stabbing a piece of chicken and popping it into her mouth. This is my chance to prove once and for all that I'm just as mature as Brian and Brittany. I'll show them, if it's the last thing I ever do.

After about twenty minutes, Julie, Molly, and Sarah came in and sat down across the dining room. They waved at the Barry family.

"Hey, look," said Todd. "The band is setting up."

Brittany whirled toward the front of the room, her eyes glowing. "Finally some real action," she said.

Beth saw Brian glance at the table where the girls were sitting. Would he ask Molly to dance? she wondered. Molly had certainly flirted with him earlier in the great room.

This is definitely my big chance, Beth thought. She slipped her mirror out of her purse and quickly checked her lipstick and hair. Then she sat up straight and looked around the room, a tiny smile playing on her lips.

Within fifteen minutes the band began to play. There were two guitars, a synthesizer, and drums. Most of the music was made up of current Top 40 tunes, but the band also mixed in some oldies to please the parents and grandparents in the audience.

"Come on, honey, let's dance," Mrs. Barry said to her husband. "It's been ages."

"But, Mom," Todd said, slouching down into his seat. "No one else is dancing yet."

"So we'll get them started," replied his mother. "I love this song. It's easy to dance to." She laughed.

Beth watched her parents head for the dance floor.

"Is this embarrassing or what?" Todd mumbled, staring at his empty plate.

"I think they're kind of cute," Brittany answered.

Beth looked around the dining room, wondering if anyone would ask her to dance. After all, she and

Keith Masterson had broken up, and she could dance with anyone she pleased. She spotted a few older boys about Brian's age. Maybe one of them would ask her.

A tall, dark-haired boy around sixteen was staring in her direction. She felt herself blush and glanced away shyly. When she looked back, she gave him a little smile. The boy got up from his table and started walking toward her. Beth's heart leapt into her throat.

He's going to ask me to dance! she thought. She didn't know whether to jump up and run to meet him halfway or hide under the table. So she held her ground, her heart beating wildly in her chest.

When he was in front of her, Beth looked up and smiled.

He didn't even notice her. "Want to dance?" he asked Brittany.

Brittany hopped up, grinning, and walked with him to the dance floor.

Let me die right now, Beth thought. She shrank into her seat, her face as red as a traffic light, and glanced around. Had anyone noticed that she had just totally humiliated herself beyond belief? Maybe she could slink off upstairs without anyone's seeing her.

Beth glanced out of the corner of her eye at Brittany, trying to figure out why the boy had picked her instead of Beth. Brittany didn't look that much older, and she was only a couple of inches taller than Beth. Maybe he likes longer hair, Beth mused, running her fingers through her own short, spiky do. Brittany's hair was the same dark brown, but it hung to her shoulders in back and waved gracefully around her face in front.

Beth looked up with a start and realized that Molly was standing next to Brian.

"Want to dance, Brian?" Molly asked.

Brian smiled. "Sure."

Beth gazed around the dining room, reminding herself that there really weren't many boys her age. And the boys who *were* her age all looked pretty immature. They were the "hot-dog skiers" Julie had mentioned. Brian and Brittany were just lucky.

Then Beth noticed a red-haired boy about her age heading for her table. Oh, no, she thought, cringing. Not a hotdogger. I don't want to dance with one of them. He'll probably stomp my feet to a pulp.

Instead the boy skirted around the table and stopped next to Todd. "Want to go to the video arcade?" he asked him.

"Sure," said Todd, hopping out of his chair. "It beats sitting around here watching a boring dance."

"That's what *I* thought," the boy agreed. The two of them headed out the door.

Beth sighed as she sat with Alicia and watched her parents, Brittany, and Brian on the dance floor.

"Hey, that was fun," said Brittany after the song was over and she and her parents had returned to the table. "Wasn't he cute? His name's Brad Jenkins, and he's from Wisconsin."

"I'm glad he asked you to dance," said Mrs. Barry. "We had a good time, too." She gazed sadly at Beth and then patted her husband's arm. "Jeff, why don't you dance with Beth?"

Beth looked up. "What!"

Brittany exploded with laughter.

"Go on, honey," her mother urged. "Dance with your father."

"Yes, Beth," Brittany teased. "Dance with your *daddy*!"

"Oh, that's okay," Beth said, glaring at her sister. "I'm having fun watching."

Please, oh, *please*, Beth thought desperately. *I don't want to dance with my own FATHER! I'd die of embarrassment!*

"Go ahead, you two," said Mrs. Barry. "I'm going to take Alicia upstairs to bed."

"Come on, Beth," her father said. "It'll be fun."

"Sure, Beth," Brittany said, grinning wickedly. "It'll be fun."

Beth didn't know what to do. She didn't want to hurt her father's feelings, but she just couldn't dance with him.

"I have a little stomachache," she lied.

"Come on." Her father pulled Beth out of her chair. "It'll do you good."

As he led her to the dance floor, Beth heard Brittany giggle. When Beth saw her sister again, Brittany was holding one hand over her mouth, trying to hold back her laughter.

It was a slow dance, so her father put one arm around her waist, placed one of her hands on his shoulder, and took her other hand.

Maybe I'll have a heart attack and die right here, Beth thought. She felt stiff and awkward as her father led her around the dance floor. Glancing over his shoulder, she saw Brian dancing with Molly. Molly was practically plastered against him. Brian looked over and grinned at Beth.

He's laughing at me, too, Beth thought. Why couldn't I have been born an only child?

When the music stopped and she started back to her seat, her face was hot and prickly. She was positive that everyone in the entire dining room was looking at her and snickering.

Julie and Sarah were sitting at her family's table when she got there. Brian and Molly followed close behind her and sat down.

"Well," said Mr. Barry, "I think I'll find Todd and then go up to the room and join your mother."

"Okay, Dad," Beth said.

What a relief, she thought. With her parents out

of the way, maybe she could blend in with the older kids.

"Want to come back, too?" her father asked, looking at Beth.

"Uh, no, thanks," Beth said. "I think I'll—just stay and listen to the music for a while."

He checked his watch. "For an hour, okay? Then you come up to the room and watch Alicia so your mother and I can come back down."

Beth started to open her mouth and say, "Why do *I* always have to be the sitter?" But she didn't want to act like an immature kid, arguing with her father in front of everyone, so she forced herself to smile. "Okay," she replied softly.

"Look after your sister," Mr. Barry told Brian and Brittany.

"Sure," Brittany said. "We'll look after our little sister, and in one hour we'll send her up to bed."

Beth was determined not to give Brittany the satisfaction of watching her get angry. She made herself look her father right in the eye. "I'll be fine, Dad."

Beth expected another snide remark from Brittany as soon as her father left, but her sister was too interested in the other kids to bother with her.

The band started playing again, and Molly turned to Brian. "Want to dance again?" she asked.

"How about sitting this one out?" Brian said.

"Oh, but Brian, this is my most *favorite* song

in the whole world," Molly pleaded, tugging his arm.

Brian laughed. "Well, I guess in that case we'd better not waste it."

As they were getting up to go to the dance floor, a man walked into the dining room, and Beth caught her breath. He was tall, tanned, muscular, and the best-looking guy she had ever seen. She quickly estimated his age to be twenty or so, too old for her, but she didn't even care. She would be happy just to *look* at this incredibly handsome guy.

Brittany had spotted him, too. In fact, Beth noticed that just about every female in the room had turned to stare at him.

He nodded cordially to people sitting at tables scattered across the room, and his gaze stopped when he looked their way. Beth watched in amazement as he waved and smiled in their direction. Julie, Sarah, and Molly returned the wave.

Brittany grabbed Julie's arm and whispered. "Who is that guy?"

"I knew that would be your next question," Julie said, laughing.

"Isn't he unbelievably good-looking?" asked Sarah.

"Incredible," answered Brittany, not moving her eyes from him even for a second. "He looks like a movie star!"

"His name is Marcel Goujon," Julie told her. "He's from France."

"He's the ski instructor here," explained Sarah. "And you should hear his accent. It's *wonderful!*"

"He's the ski instructor, is he?" asked Brittany, a smile creeping across her face. Beth could guess what was going through her sister's mind.

"Uh-huh," said Julie. "We take lessons every chance we get."

Brittany grinned. "Surely you're getting too good for lessons by now."

Sarah shrugged. "It takes a long time to learn to ski well. Lots of people take lessons over and over again."

Beth smiled to herself. Probably some people did take ski lessons over and over again, but she wasn't fooled by Julie, Sarah, and Molly. They wanted to be close to Marcel.

"Is Marcel married?" asked Brittany.

"Nope," Julie said.

"Great!" exclaimed Brittany. She still hadn't taken her eyes off Marcel, who was now sitting with a couple at a table near the far wall.

"Who's he sitting with?" Brittany was craning her neck to see across the crowded room.

"Mr. and Mrs. Martin," said Julie. "They own the resort. He comes in here several times a week to have dinner with them."

"Do you think he'll ask anyone to dance?" asked Brittany.

Julie sighed. "He never does."

"But we've seen plenty of girls ask him," added Sarah.

"Really?" Brittany said. "Have *you* asked him?"

Sarah chuckled. "No. We're still working up our nerve."

"But does he dance with the girls who ask him?" Brittany pressed.

"Yes," said Julie. "But I think he's just being polite."

Just then Brad Jenkins, the boy who had danced with Brittany earlier, approached and asked her to dance again.

"Sure," Brittany said. But Beth noticed that she glanced over at Marcel as she made her way to the dance floor.

It was a fast dance, and Brittany really threw herself into it. Beth knew Brittany was an excellent dancer, but she hadn't realized just how good her sister really was. Brittany swung around and waved her arms in the air and really looked great.

Beth noticed that Brittany moved a little toward the far side of the dance floor, and Brad followed. Seconds later Brittany took a few more steps to the side, and Brad followed again.

Then it dawned on Beth what her sister was

doing. *She's moving closer to Marcel! She wants to get his attention with her dancing!*

Well, that should do it, Beth thought. If Brittany's dancing won't get Marcel to notice her, nothing will.

Beth sat up as tall as she could and was able to see Marcel. He and the Martins were talking. Once Marcel looked up, seeming to watch someone on the dance floor.

It was Brittany, of course. Who else?

Beth sighed and rested her elbows on the table, her chin in her hands. This is the crowning blow, she thought. Brittany gets a bed all to herself, she doesn't have to go back to the room early, and she doesn't have to baby-sit Alicia. And now she's got the attention of the most handsome man in the whole world. It just isn't fair!

Frowning, Beth checked her watch. Her father had left only ten minutes ago. That meant she could stay for another fifty minutes, if she wanted to.

But why bother? she thought gloomily. Everyone will dance except me, everyone will have fun except me, everyone will talk and be included in the conversation. Except me. There's no point in hanging around. It's just too depressing to be left out. Not to mention embarrassing.

She faked a yawn. "I'm pretty tired," she told Julie. "Guess I'll go upstairs and let my folks come down for a while."

"Okay," Julie said faintly. "See you tomorrow."

Beth sighed. She got up and headed upstairs to her room, where she could have her own dream about whirling around the dance floor with Marcel Goujon.

CHAPTER

4

"*I* can't believe I'm going to learn to ski!" Brittany said the next morning. She had been primping before the mirror for almost an hour already, and it wasn't even time for breakfast.

"You mean you can't wait to hang around Marcel," Beth mumbled under her breath.

She was in no mood to put up with Brittany this morning. She hadn't fallen asleep for hours last night, alternating between reliving the embarrassing scenes in the dining room and wondering what was going on at home during the first night of Winter Carnival. She had memorized the carnival schedule before she left home. Last night there had been toboggan races down Spyglass Hill and a snowman-building contest. She knew that everyone had been there—except her. And they'd probably all had a ball. In all of that excitement, had anyone missed her? she wondered. Had anyone even noticed that she wasn't there? The thought made her shiver.

After breakfast the Barrys made a stop at the ski shop, renting skis, boots, and poles. Beth and Todd trailed behind the others as they clomped toward the slopes with their skis over their shoulders, Beth suddenly stopped and plunged her free hand into her jacket pocket.

"Oh, no," she whispered, pulling a red leather change purse out and shaking her head angrily.

"Hey, what's in there?" asked Todd. "Money," he added in a satisfied tone. "You always keep money in there, don't you?"

"Don't get any big ideas," Beth warned. "I'm not going to spend it. It's the money I'm saving for our trip to London over spring break to visit Christie. I just didn't want to leave it home while we're here. Someone could break in and steal it."

"So why did you pull it out now?" asked Todd.

"I just remembered that it was in my jacket. I meant to hide it in my room while we're skiing. I'd die if I lost it on the slopes."

"Hey, I'll keep it for you," Todd said, grinning slyly.

"Oh, no you don't." Beth pushed it deep into her

pocket and zippered it in. Then she patted the pocket and said, "I'll take my chances right here."

As they hurried on to catch up with the others, Beth felt a tingle of anticipation for the trip to England during the school vacation in the spring. Each family had agreed to pay airfare if the girls would save their own spending money. It was going to be tough to accumulate enough in the few weeks left before the trip, and Beth was determined not to let her money out of her sight.

When Beth and Todd reached the meeting area for beginner lessons at the bottom of the slope, Mr. and Mrs. Barry had already dropped Alicia off at the school for tiny tots and were heading for the lifts themselves, since they already knew how to ski.

Todd had skied before, too, and he stopped short of the beginners' area and said to Beth, "Hey, I told my friends I'd meet them by the lift. See you later."

Beth waved good-bye to Todd and went to join Brian and Brittany, who were standing with Julie, Molly, and Sarah. As usual, no one noticed her. Brian was deep in conversation with Molly, and Brittany was scanning the crowd on the slopes.

Julie giggled. "If you're looking for Marcel, he's on his way." She pointed to a figure in a red ski jacket walking toward them carrying skis over his shoulder.

"Ohhhhh," Brittany breathed. "He's even better-looking in the daylight."

"He sure is," agreed Sarah.

"Okay, everyone, we're ready to start," Marcel called out when he reached the area a moment later. The skiers stopped talking and gave him their attention. "First, let me eeentroduce myself. I am Marcel Goujon, your eeenstruc-tair. Call me Marcel."

"His accent is sooo fantastic," Brittany whispered to Sarah.

"Tell me about it," Sarah whispered back.

There were about fifteen people in the class, Beth noticed as she glanced around. Their ages varied from a man who looked to be in his sixties to a few elementary school kids. Again, however, there wasn't anyone Beth's age.

"Ze first thing we need to learn," Marcel was saying, "is to put on ze skis."

"That should be helpful for skiing!" said Brittany loudly. Julie giggled.

Everyone turned to look at Brittany, and she grinned at Marcel.

He smiled back and continued. "First you'll need to clean ze snow from your boots. Use ze tip of your pole. Then step into ze bindings, toe first. Watch. I will show you."

The skiers crowded near to watch. Brittany was almost touching his shoulder. Beth followed Marcel's

instructions and felt her boots click into the bindings. She slid her skis back and forth on the snow to
test them. They felt tight.

"I think mine are loose," Julie called out. "Can
you help me please, Marcel?"

"*Mais oui*," Marcel replied. He glided gracefully
over to her and leaned down to check her skis. Julie
rolled her eyes in a mock swoon. Some of the girls in
the group looked jealous, including Brittany.

After he had helped Julie and a few others with
their skis, Marcel said, "Now let's learn how to fall."

"I thought that came naturally," commented Brittany. Everyone laughed.

"*Oui*, it does, but there is a right way and a wrong
way to fall," Marcel answered. "It's important to remember: Do *not* tense up when you fall. Keep your
skis together and fall to ze side and backward a little.
Always try to keep your skis downhill."

Beth loved hearing Marcel talk. His accent was
fabulous. But she tried to concentrate on what he
was saying. If the rest of the vacation was going to be
crummy, at least she would learn to ski.

"Okay, let's say you have just fallen," Marcel said.
"Ze next thing to do is learn how to get back up.
Everyone sit on ze ground."

The class did as they were told.

He explained how to use the poles to pull up in
the snow and then demonstrated the technique. He

sprang to his feet with one effortless movement. "Voilà! Nothing to it. Now you do it."

The skiers followed his directions, laughing at how awkward they felt. Beth concentrated on following Marcel's example and managed to pull herself to her feet. Pleased, she looked around at the others, who were grunting and struggling and gradually getting up. Brittany kept pulling and pushing and plopping back down.

"Marcel!" cried Brittany, falling back one more time.

With a feeling of disgust Beth watched Marcel help her sister. Brittany was obviously pretending to be helpless just to get his attention.

"If you should land with your skis crossed," Marcel continued, "or pointed in opposite directions—"

"Ouch! That sounds painful," called out Brittany.

"It sure does," said Sarah. The rest of the class murmured agreement.

Marcel smiled patiently and went on. "Roll onto your back and lift both skis in ze air. Then you can swing them so they are parallel and put them on ze snow again." He looked at Brittany. "It's not as bad as it sounds," he said. "Most of ze time you do not get hurt."

His attention made Brittany beam. Beth felt like throwing up.

"Now let's try walking," Marcel said. "It's not really walking, but gliding instead."

He taught them how to slide along in the snow and coordinate their ski poles with the right, left, right, left movement of their legs. He also taught them how to turn around on their skis, and how to do a sidestep climb up a hill.

"Okay, I believe you're ready to try a little hill," said Marcel. "Follow me to ze bunny slope."

They ski-walked behind Marcel to the smallest slope in the area. Actually, Beth decided, it was more of an incline than a hill. It was not much taller than she was, and it ran gradually down at a gentle slope.

"We'll use ze towrope," Marcel explained. He stopped near a small wooden structure from which a rope, about waist high, moved slowly up the slope to another structure at the top.

Beth watched as two skiers who had gotten there ahead of the class grasped the rope and let it pull them up the hill.

"Put your skis into ze groove in ze snow, and gently squeeze ze rope until it pulls you along. Don't squeeze tightly or put your weight on it. It will not support you. Watch. I will show you."

He grabbed the rope and squeezed gently, and it pulled him up the hill. He skied back down. "Now I will help you. Who is first?"

Brittany's hand shot up. "I'll go first!"

"Fine. Come." He beckoned to her, and she glided over to him, grinning from ear to ear.

Marcel put his arms around Brittany from behind and helped her position her hands on the rope. Brittany stood, not paying attention to his instruction, but gazing back into his eyes. Marcel asked, "Ready?"

She didn't answer for a moment, but continued to stare at him, her mouth hanging open a little. Beth was so embarrassed, she had to look away. Brittany was making a complete fool of herself!

"Mademoiselle? Ready?" Marcel asked Brittany again.

"Oh!" Brittany snapped to attention. "Yes! Yes, I'm ready."

"Okay, hold on. Keep your skis parallel to ze rope. We'll see you at ze top," Marcel said.

"Bye," Brittany said in a little voice. She gripped the towrope, and as it started pulling her, she glanced over her shoulder with a look of panic on her face.

"Watch ze top of ze slope!" Marcel yelled to her.

"Oh!" Brittany nearly fell, but managed to keep herself upright.

Marcel smiled and watched her till she reached the top of the incline and slid off to one side. "*Très bien!*" he called up to her, clapping his hands.

From where she stood at the bottom of the slope, Beth could see the pleasure in Brittany's face. Brittany beamed, then took a dramatic bow. Beth shook her head and wished she could crawl into a hole somewhere. How could Marcel be attracted to Brittany when she was acting so stupid?

Beth was the last one to ride the towrope up the slope. She forced herself to pay attention to what she was doing. She followed Marcel's instructions carefully, so she wouldn't look as idiotic as Brittany had, and she made it up the hill without an incident.

At the top of the slope Marcel announced that the next thing they would do was learn to "snowplow." He explained that it was the easiest way to control their downhill speed. He showed the skiers how to put the tips of the skis together and the tails out to form an inverted V.

"This will slow you down," he explained. "When you want to go faster, pull your skis back into ze parallel position and continue downhill. Then when you're going too fast again, put ze tips together." He demonstrated the snowplow technique, slowing and speeding up as he skied down the slope.

"Wow," said Brittany when he had returned. "Marcel, you're such an *expert*! You make it look so *easy*!"

"Would you like to try first?" asked Marcel. "It's not hard."

Brittany practically dove at him. "You bet!"

He glided with her to the edge of the incline.

"Oh, this is scary!" she said, putting her hand on his arm.

"You'll be fine." Marcel spoke in a soothing voice.

"What if I fall?" Brittany responded helplessly.

"Remember how I taught you to fall," Marcel answered. "To ze side and backward."

"Oh, yeah," she said. "Okay. Well, here goes."

Beth was almost afraid to look, and she squinted as she watched her sister push off the slope and start down.

"Ohhhhhhh!" Brittany called out.

"When you feel yourself going too fast, put your ski tips together," Marcel shouted.

Brittany made a sudden, jerky movement and fell flat on her seat, sliding for several feet before coming to a stop. Marcel skied to her and helped her up. Then he said something to her that Beth couldn't hear, and Brittany started again. When she finally reached the bottom of the slope, she cheered loudly. Marcel laughed.

One by one the rest of the group tried the snowplow. Beth found to her surprise that she could do it pretty easily. She actually enjoyed it and tried curving back and forth across the slope. When she reached the bottom without falling once, Marcel approached her.

"Good job," he said. "Your size is good for skiing. You are small and light. That is very good."

Beth smiled at him. She turned to see if Brittany had heard Marcel's compliment, but of course she hadn't. She was huddled with Julie and Sarah, undoubtedly telling them about her own experience with Marcel a few minutes ago.

The class continued to practice on the bunny slope for the rest of the lesson. Brittany, Julie, and Sarah are acting so stupid, Beth thought. They kept falling and laughing loudly and asking Marcel for help.

Molly played the helpless female, too, only her target wasn't Marcel. It was Brian.

"Oh, Brian, can you help me up?"

"Oh, Brian, this is so hard! Would you show me how to do it."

"Brian! You're so strong!"

Beth was disgusted with all of them. When the lesson was over and they were back at the lodge, she sat by the fireplace in the great room listening to Brittany and the other girls gush about "Magnificent Marcel." They schemed about asking him to dance that night and inviting him to the game room to play pool.

Beth wished she could join in the conversation, even though she thought the girls were acting like jerks. She thought Marcel was wonderful, too, but she didn't want to say anything. The older girls would make fun of her. If only The Fabulous Five were here, she thought, they'd understand how I feel. We'd be laughing and talking and having fun, too.

Beth sighed and felt a lump forming in her chest. But The Fabulous Five weren't here. Katie, Jana, and Melanie were at home, having a blast at Winter Carnival, Christie was having the time of her life in London, and she was stuck here. Even though she was with her whole family, and there were other people around, Beth was still lonely. And there was nothing she could do about it. She had no friends here, no one she could talk to. What a crummy vacation.

When Beth walked out of the great room to go up to her room, no one even noticed.

CHAPTER

5

I wonder what Katie and Melanie and Jana are doing right this minute? Beth thought sadly as she made her way back to her room. They're probably somewhere together, talking about what a great time they had last night.

Closing the door behind her, she started taking off her ski jacket when her hand brushed against the pocket where she'd put her small leather purse.

"Maybe it wouldn't hurt if I spent a *little*," she whispered. "Just enough for one short phone call to my friends. How much could that cost, anyway? Especially if we only talked for a couple of minutes."

She pursed her lips and eyed the telephone on the

table between the beds. Then she picked up the instruction card lying beside the phone.

To make a long-distance call, dial 9 + area code and number. The call will be billed to your room.

That sounds easy, she thought. I'll just explain to Mom and Dad that I needed to talk to my friends, and then I'll give them the money to pay for the call when we check out and get the bill. A sudden memory stopped her for an instant. It was the time she had gotten into a lot of trouble with her parents over money when she borrowed Shawnie Pendergast's credit card to buy clothes. But this is different, she assured herself.

Beth plopped down on her bed and reached for the phone. This is going to be so much fun, she thought. But her hand stopped in midair.

"Gosh," she said. "Which one of them should I call?"

She thought for a moment, deciding on Jana. Then she picked up the receiver, dialed 9 and then the area code and Jana's number.

It rang only once before a cheery voice said, "Hello."

Beth blinked in astonishment and then looked at her watch. She had expected Jana's mother and her stepfather to be at work, but it was after five in the afternoon. "Oh, hi, Mrs. Pink. Is Jana there?"

"Beth? Is that you?" asked Mrs. Pinkerton. "I thought you were away on a big ski vacation."

"I am," said Beth. "I'm calling long-distance."

"I see. Well, Jana isn't here right now," Mrs. Pinkerton told her. "She's at the dentist. I hope nothing's wrong."

"Oh," gulped Beth. "No, nothing's wrong, but I'd better hang up. Thanks, Mrs. Pink. Just tell her I said hi."

Beth sighed as she hung up. She would have to pay for the call, and she hadn't even talked to Jana. It was a shame to spend money and get nothing for it, she thought, looking at the phone again. Surely, she reasoned, if she made one more call, she'd catch someone at home.

This time she dialed Melanie's number.

"Hello. Edwards residence. *Mr.* Jeffy speaking."

"Hi, Jeffy. This is Beth. Will you get Melanie? And please hurry. I'm calling long-distance."

"Can't," Jeffy replied matter-of-factly.

"Why not?"

"She's not here. Bye."

The dial tone rang in Beth's ear before she could ask him to take a message. "Six-year-olds," she muttered in exasperation.

Beth chewed on her lip and thought again. Two calls to pay for, and she still hadn't talked to one of her friends. "It's incredible!" she exclaimed. Still, she would have to call Katie to make spending all this money worthwhile.

"But I *can't* spend any more money," she whispered. On the other hand, she knew Mrs. Pinkerton would tell Jana she had called, and Jeffy was a goofy six-year-old, but she was sure he would tell Melanie, too. Katie will be hurt if I don't call her, Beth reasoned.

She took a deep breath and tried again. One, two, three rings. At least I won't have to pay for a call if no one answers, she thought. Five, six, the ringing stopped.

"Hello. You have reached the Shannon residence. Neither Willie nor Katie can come to the phone right now, but if you will leave your name and number after the beep . . ."

Beth slammed down the phone. "Not the answering machine!" she cried.

She threw herself across her bed, burying her face in a pillow. Three long-distance calls, and not one of her friends had been at home. Suddenly she raised her head and moaned, "And I didn't leave a message for Katie! She won't even know I called!"

Todd bragged all during dinner about how he had skied some of the tougher slopes with "the guys."

"Man, you should have seen me bombing down those mountains. Me and the guys probably broke some speed records while we were at it." He grinned at Beth. "I bet things were pretty hairy on the bunny slopes, too, huh?"

Beth rolled her eyes in disgust. "Grow up," she growled. Even Jeffy Edwards acted more mature than Todd.

"Todd," Mr. Barry warned, "you take it easy. I watched some of your friends skiing today, and they're pretty advanced."

"So am I!" Todd replied, obviously insulted.

"Yes, you are," Mr. Barry agreed. "But just be careful."

Beth smirked at her brother, thinking that he deserved to be reprimanded by their dad. At the same time she secretly wished she were good enough to ski some of the bigger slopes. Marcel had pointed out the warning markers and explained their color coding to alert skiers to the differences in difficulty—green for beginner slopes, black for intermediate slopes, and red for the more dangerous expert slopes. What fun it would be to be really good like the skiers she had watched streaking down the mountain with plumes of snow spraying up behind them.

She bet Christie would be a good skier. Christie was an expert tennis player, and did everything else just as well. It was sad that Christie's family had moved to England. Beth missed her a lot.

Beth glanced at her sister. Brittany hadn't made any rude comments about Beth's hanging around with her and her friends for a while. In fact Brittany hadn't even seemed to notice her.

After dinner Beth's parents went off for a walk in the snow with Alicia, and Julie, Molly, and Sarah came over to the table. Brittany was busy looking for her new crush, Marcel, so Beth had become invisible again.

"If Marcel isn't here in fifteen minutes," said Julie, "we should go and see if he's in the game room."

"Are you really going to ask him to dance?" Sarah asked Brittany, her eyes wide with excitement.

"Sure. Why not?" Brittany answered confidently. "Don't you think he'd dance with me?"

"Absolutely," said Sarah. "I'd never have the nerve, but *you* are such a great dancer, Brittany. I bet he'd love to dance with you."

A smile crept across Brittany's face. "Maybe I'll ask him on a slow song."

Julie looked awestruck. "I'd give *anything* for a slow dance with Marcel."

Just then Brad Jenkins, the boy from Wisconsin, stepped up to their table. "Brittany, would you like to dance?"

"Not this time, thanks," Brittany replied with a

definite lack of interest in her voice. "I'm really tired after all the skiing today."

Brad looked so disappointed that Beth blurted out without thinking, "I'll dance with you."

She was immediately sorry she'd opened her mouth, because everyone at the table looked at her. Brittany snickered.

Brad looked as if he were going to drop dead on the spot. "Sure, okay," he mumbled.

Stupid, stupid! Beth raged at herself. *Why didn't you keep your big mouth shut!* She got up stiffly and didn't look at him all the way to the dance floor. It was a slow dance, and Brad put his arm around her waist and took her hand in his.

"I like this song," he said.

"Me, too," replied Beth.

They didn't speak for the rest of the dance. When the music stopped, Brad said, "Thanks for dancing with me."

"Sure," Beth answered.

He turned and walked back to his own table. The last thing Beth wanted to do at that moment was face Brittany's sarcasm, so she walked straight out of the dining room and into the great room.

Brad had seemed like a nice person. Unfortunately it was Brittany he was interested in, and Brittany obviously thought she was too sophisticated for him. Her silly comment about being too tired to dance certainly wasn't true. If Marcel had asked her to dance, she would have danced all night!

Crossing the great room, Beth headed for the game room. In the doorway she stopped in her tracks. There, playing pool with another guy about his age, was Marcel.

Beth entered the room and slipped onto a couch along the wall. There were a dozen or so people in the room, playing board games or Ping-Pong, or watching TV.

She tried watching the movie on the TV, but it didn't hold her attention. Her eyes kept flicking back to Marcel. When she and Keith Masterson had broken up a couple of months ago, she had convinced herself that she'd had it with boys, at least for a while. And of course Marcel was definitely too old for her. But still . . . She couldn't help thinking how much fun it would be to have something *interesting* to tell her friends when she got back home.

"Hi, Beth." The voice beside her startled her. It was Molly's.

"Oh, hi, Molly," said Beth. "Where's Brian?"

"He went up to his room to get his coat," replied Molly, smiling. "I invited him to take a walk in the moonlight."

"That sounds nice," said Beth.

Molly sat down next to her and whispered, "You should go tell your sister that Marcel's in here."

"Oh, yeah," Beth answered, but she had absolutely no intention of doing it.

"Beth," Molly said in a low, confidential voice. "I've been trying to talk to you privately since last night." She laughed a little, sounding nervous. "Tell me about Brian."

Beth turned to her. "What do you mean?"

"I want to know all about him."

"Well . . ." Beth shrugged. "He's seventeen—"

"Does he have a girlfriend at home?" Molly asked. That was obviously what she really wanted to know.

"Not really," said Beth. "I mean, he dates, but he doesn't have a steady girlfriend."

Molly looked relieved. "Oh, that's great. And when is his birthday?"

"In July," Beth said. "The second."

"Oh." Molly sounded disappointed. "I guess it's not coming up anytime soon."

"No, I guess not." Boy, Beth thought, Molly really has it bad for Brian.

"What kinds of things does he like in a girl?" Molly asked.

The question caught Beth off guard. "Well, . . . I guess he likes girls who have the same qualities *you* do. He sure seems to like you."

Molly's face lit up. "Did he tell you that?" she asked anxiously.

"Well, no," Beth admitted, "but he doesn't have to. You two are together all the time, so he must like you."

"Hmmm," Molly said frowning. "Well, I mean, what do you think attracts Brian? Does he like girls who are athletic, or gorgeous, or talented—"

"All of the above." Beth laughed.

"Well, um, does he—" Molly stammered.

"What?"

"Well, what I mean is—" Molly hesitated a moment, "do you think he prefers girls who have great—uh, bodies or superior minds?"

Beth smirked. "Don't all guys like great bodies?"

Molly shrugged and started to ask something else, but just then Brian came into the room.

"Here you are," he said to Molly.

She got up quickly. "Well, Beth, it was fun talking to you." She looked at Brian. "Ready for our walk?"

Brian nodded, and Molly tucked her arm in his and gave a little squeeze.

Wow, thought Beth as she watched them leave, is Molly ever hooked!

After they had gone, she suddenly felt lonely again. If only her parents had let her bring a friend.

"Hello," said a deep voice.

Beth looked up and caught her breath. Marcel was

walking around the pool table, looking at her. *And he had spoken to her.*

"Hi," said Beth. She could feel her cheeks getting hot.

"Was ze ski lesson today your first?" he asked.

Beth nodded. "Yes."

"You did very well," he responded. "Did you enjoy it?"

"Oh, yes. I liked it a lot. Thanks."

"Good," Marcel said. "You'll be even better tomorrow."

He went back to shooting pool, and Beth sat there stunned. *He talked to me!* she thought. *He didn't have to, either. He was in the middle of a game of pool!*

She didn't have time to enjoy the moment, though, because just then Brittany, Julie, and Sarah walked in. They put their heads together and started whispering as soon as they saw Marcel.

Well, that's that, Beth thought with disgust. Marcel won't be talking to *me* anymore, that's for sure. Brittany and her friends will monopolize him.

Sure enough, the three teenagers strolled over to Marcel's pool table to watch him play. They stood so close, he had to adjust his position to keep from hitting one of them with his cue.

"Good shot!" Brittany called out as Marcel sank a ball. Marcel nodded in recognition of the compliment.

"Gosh, he can ski *and* play pool!" Julie gushed so loudly, he was sure to hear.

Brittany beamed in his direction. "He's good at everything he does."

Beth watched Marcel to see how he would react. At first his face didn't change. Then he smiled at Brittany. "Not everything."

"Oh, you're too modest," Brittany said, giving him her best smile.

Marcel continued to play and talk to his friend while the girls flirted with him.

"After your game," Brittany said, "would you and your friend like to come back and dance with us?"

Beth saw Julie's eyes widen in surprise at Brittany's nerve.

Marcel checked his watch. "*Oui*. We have time for a dance or two, don't we, Jake?"

"Sure," replied Jake. "The movie doesn't start till nine."

"A movie?" Brittany gushed. "What're you going to see?"

"It's an old movie on TV," Marcel said. "Humphrey Bogart."

"I *love* Bogart!" Brittany cried, and Beth knew she was hoping for an invitation.

"Gosh, me, too," chimed in Julie. "Don't you, Sarah?"

"Definitely," agreed Sarah.

Marcel grinned at the girls. His gaze shifted to Beth, and he said, "And you, mademoiselle, do you also love Bogart?" He winked.

"Sure," Beth said, "he's all right."

Marcel smiled at her, then turned back to Brittany. "A dance would be very nice."

"Great," said Brittany. "We'll be in the dining room waiting for you."

She and her friends headed toward the door, but just before she made her exit, she took two steps out of the way toward Beth and hissed, *"Isn't it past your bedtime, little sister?"*

Then she flounced out the door after her girlfriends.

CHAPTER

6

*B*eth had no intention of going to bed. Not with Brittany and the others headed back to the dining room and Marcel still here in the game room. She wasn't going to do anything silly or theatrical to attract his attention, of course. She would just sit here, acting incredibly mature, and see what happened.

"Geez! What are you doing in *here*? I've been looking all over for you."

Todd came rushing into the game room followed by two of his skiing companions. Both were about Todd's height, but one had curly red hair and a sunburned face, and the other one was a sandy blond and as slim as a toothpick. Todd was smiling so sweetly that Beth was immediately suspicious.

"What do you want?" she grumbled.

Todd raised his arms in mock surrender. "Not much, and I'll pay you back. I promise."

"That's right," said the red-haired boy. "We'll get the money from our parents before we go home and give it to Todd to give to you."

"What!" shrieked Beth. "You guys actually want to borrow money from me? You've got to be kidding."

"No, we aren't," Todd said earnestly. Nodding toward the other two, he continued, "This is Jason, and he's Mike. They're great guys. Honest. We only need a few bucks, and we said we'd pay you back."

Beth narrowed her eyes. All three boys were looking at her with angelic expressions on their faces. Did they honestly expect her to say yes?

"Sorry," she answered with a dismissive wave of her hand. "I didn't bring much spending money, and I certainly don't have any extra money to loan you."

"Oh, yes you do," Todd said excitedly. "It's in your ski jacket. The stuff you're saving for England. Jason and Mike and I will definitely pay you back. I promise. Come on, Beth. We need it for the video games."

Beth exploded off the sofa and stood nose to nose

with Todd. "If you think I'm going to loan that money to you, you little twerp, you've got another thing coming! I wouldn't trust you and your hot-dog ski friends with my money for five seconds flat!"

Suddenly she was aware of a deep-throated chuckle coming from across the room. It was Marcel, and he was shaking his head and laughing softly. Beth froze. She had forgotten he was there.

"Siblings," he said, smiling at Beth. "They are ze same ze world over. But believe me, when you two grow up, you'll feel much different about each other."

Beth stared at Marcel, his words ringing in her ears. *When you two grow up.* Did he see her as a child, too? What was the matter with him? Couldn't he see that it was Todd who was behaving like a little kid?

Marcel turned back to his game of pool. Beth stood there for a moment, wondering what to do. Then she squared her shoulders and pulled herself up to her full height. Mustering her courage, she smiled at Todd and his friends and said in her most dignified voice, "Well, I think I'll turn in now. See you all in the morning."

Then she disappeared out the door.

"Today we will try a slightly steeper hill," Marcel said when the class assembled again the next morn-

ing. "You all learned ze snowplow very well yesterday, and I think you're ready."

An excited murmur ran through the class. Beth
was excited, too, but she was also nervous. Skiing
had been fun and almost easy on the bunny slope. A
steeper hill sounded scary.

Beth followed Marcel along with the rest of the
skiers. Of course, Brittany, Julie, and Sarah were
right at the front of the group, making cute remarks
to him. Occasionally he would turn and smile or say
something clever back to them. No matter what he
said, though, the girls giggled wildly and flirted
with him all the more.

Marcel led the group to a slope, which Beth could
see was definitely steeper than the one they had
skied yesterday. A small building sat about a hun-
dred feet away. It had the same rustic look as the
lodge, only it was smaller and built above the snow
on heavy stone legs at each corner.

"Oh, Marcel, what an adorable little house," Brittany gushed. "Is that where you live?"

She turned around to acknowledge the laughter of
some of the class. Beth wanted to burrow into a
snowbank and hide with embarrassment.

"No," Marcel answered patiently. "That is where
ze ski lift equipment is stored during ze summer.
Now, if you will grab ze towrope, we'll meet at ze

top of ze slope." Then he gestured for Brittany to start up the hill first. "After you, mademoiselle."

Brittany giggled. "Why, thank you, kind sir!" Then she grabbed the towrope and rode up the hill with the rest of the class following.

"I want you to try ze snowplow on this slope first," Marcel said when the class had gathered around him. "It will be more of a challenge for you."

He turned to Beth. "Mademoiselle, would you like to go first today?"

"Oh, uh, sure," replied Beth, her face getting hot. "I'll try."

"You'll do splendidly," said Marcel. "If you fall, don't be embarrassed."

Beth grinned at Marcel, even though Brittany was shooting daggers at her. "I'll probably fall."

From the top of the hill the slope looked even steeper than it had from below. Beth's heart was pounding, partly because she was first and everybody was watching, and partly because Marcel seemed to expect good things from her.

She pushed off with her poles and started snowplowing down. It was fun, and she felt a thrill run up her back as she let herself pick up speed. Then she tried making slow turns to the right and then to the left.

Suddenly the run was over. Beth snowplowed to a

stop and looked back up the slope, beaming. She had made it all the way to the bottom without falling. She felt like cheering and jumping up and down, but she didn't. After all, she didn't want to look foolish or childish in front of Marcel.

"Excellent!" Marcel called from the top. "That is exactly ze way to do it!"

He turned to the other skiers, and Beth could tell by his gestures that he was telling them to follow Beth's example. Beth let out a deep breath. Skiing was fun. For what seemed like the first time since she had gotten to Stony Lookout, she was actually enjoying herself.

When Brittany skied down a few minutes later, Beth thought her older sister might really be trying to do her best on this hill. Beth decided, with a certain amount of satisfaction, that maybe Brittany didn't want her little sister to upstage her in front of Marcel.

Next it was an older man's turn. Beth had learned his name was Charles, and even though he joked about his lack of skill as a skier, Beth had noticed that he plunged in with more energy than most of the skiers half his age.

"Here goes nothing!" Charles shouted as he started down the slope with a big grin on his face.

But about halfway down, he began to wobble.

Beth gasped as his arms and legs flung out wildly, and he fell and tumbled in the snow.

"Charles!" Beth called out. "Are you okay?"

Charles didn't answer.

Marcel sprang into action, shooting straight down the slope like an arrow, spraying snow as he made a whirling stop beside Charles. Marcel quickly took off his skis and planted them upright in an X on the slope above Charles.

Beth and the others watched breathlessly as Marcel bent over Charles. The two men talked, and Marcel touched Charles's leg. Then to everyone's relief, Marcel helped Charles to his feet. A few minutes later Charles skied the rest of the way to the bottom on his own.

When a cheer went up, Charles grinned from ear to ear. "Gee, if I'd known that falling would get me so much attention, I would have done a lot more of it."

Everyone laughed.

When the rest of the skiers had taken their turn, Marcel said that they would spend most of the lesson here, practicing on the new slope. After a few more successful runs, Beth relaxed even more and experimented with making turns and stopping. She found she loved skiing and feeling the cold air in her face. She also loved looking around at the snow and the majestic mountains that towered above her.

I'm glad I'm here, she thought. Even if there isn't anyone my age to share it with.

As she grabbed the towrope for her sixth ride up the slope, Brittany jumped into line right behind her.

Beth was feeling so good that she turned around and gave her sister a silly smile.

"Beth, you're such a show-off," Brittany complained.

Beth's smile faded. "Who, me? I'm not showing off!"

"Just because you're catching on to some of the stuff Marcel's teaching us, don't think he's interested in *you*!"

"Get real, Brittany," Beth called back over her shoulder. "It never crossed my mind that—"

Suddenly Beth lost her grip on the rope. She felt herself slide backward—into Brittany, who screamed and fell down—and then into Julie, who crumpled in the snow—and into Sarah, who was behind her.

Beth panicked. She was totally out of control, flying down the slope backward, knocking people over as if they were dominoes. With a sudden lunge to the side, she threw herself out of the towrope tracks just in time to avoid toppling the next person.

But now, she was careening down the hill frontward with the storage house looming in front of her.

She tried snowplowing, but the snow under her skis had turned to ice, and there was no way she could stop. She was speeding faster and faster, and the building was growing larger and larger as she raced toward it.

Suddenly, as she braced to smack into the building, her reflexes took over. She went limp and threw herself to the side and backward the way Marcel had taught her, and slid feetfirst between the pilings and on under the building.

She came to a stop, flat on her back and her nose nearly touching the underside of the building.

"Am I okay?" she murmured, raising her head a little. She did a quick inventory of her arms and legs, wiggling each one to make sure it was still attached and working. Everything was, and she let out a sigh of relief.

Then she heard someone yelling, "Beth! Beth!" and the horrible reality of what had just happened sank in. She had just knocked down part of her ski class, had schussed down the hill like a hotdogger, and had landed under the storage house! It was the most embarrassing moment of her entire life, and the last thing in the world she *ever* wanted to do was crawl out from under the building. She wondered whether, if she stayed quiet, everybody would go away and leave her to her misery.

She heard boots tromping toward her in the snow.

"Beth? Are you okay?"

It was Charles. She tipped her head up and saw him on his knees, peering at her through the opening between the snow and the floor of the house.

"Yeah," she said weakly, feeling a sudden spurt of tears in her eyes. "I'm fine."

Charles's face disappeared. "She's okay!" he shouted to the others, and a cheer went up.

Beth's skis had come loose, and she managed to turn over and crawl out from under the house, dragging the skis behind her. Hands reached for her and helped her up, and everyone crowded around, asking her if she was sure she was okay.

Marcel had been at the top of the hill when the accident happened. He quickly skied down and pushed through the circle of skiers gathered around Beth. "Are you all right, mademoiselle?"

"Sure, I'm fine," she mumbled. Actually her head was throbbing, and she wasn't sure how steady her legs would be. But she was too humiliated to admit it.

"You are a very smart young lady," Marcel assured her. "It was quick thinking to duck under ze storage house. *Très bien.*"

Quick thinking? Beth blinked in surprise. Was he just saying that to make her feel better? Still, she thought, it had been a pretty dramatic performance, if she did say so herself.

Slowly a sly smile spread across her face. "Thanks," she said to Marcel. And in a louder voice, she added, "Just thought that since I was falling anyway, I'd do something to entertain the crowd."

Bowing theatrically to the sound of both laughter and applause, she headed to the end of the lift line for another turn on the slope.

CHAPTER

7

*A*fter the lesson Marcel instructed the class to spend the rest of the day practicing the techniques they had learned. Brian, Molly, Brittany, Julie, and Sarah went off without a word to Beth, but that suited her fine. She rode the towrope to the top of the hill and enjoyed being alone to really concentrate on turning and stopping. Sometimes, though, she couldn't help thinking about Winter Carnival. She sighed as she remembered the beautiful ice sculpture of a snowbird that had stood in the middle of the park and how kids from Wakeman had congregated there to talk and laugh. I'll try to call one of The Fabulous Five again later, she thought. I just have to find out what's going on.

As she stood in the lift line after her fourth run, she heard Todd calling her name.

"Hey, Beth! Wait up when you get to the top, and we'll ski down with you!"

Beth's heart sank as she saw Todd waving from the end of the line, because Jason and Mike were with him. "Just what I need," she muttered.

"We watched your last run, and you're looking good," Jason said, when the boys caught up with her at the top.

"That's right," agreed Mike. "A couple more days and you'll be ready for The Jaws of Death."

Beth laughed good-naturedly, but deep down she suspected that they were just buttering her up so that they could ask her for a loan again.

"If you want to go a little faster, just bend your knees a bit," offered Jason.

Beth looked questioningly at Todd.

"Try it," said Todd. "I told you these guys are okay."

"If you say so," Beth murmured as she pushed off and started her run down the slope. The boys started down, too, Todd on her left and Jason and Mike on her right.

"Like this," called out Mike. He crouched slightly and sped ahead of her.

Beth took a deep breath and bent her knees. She immediately picked up a little speed. It was fun, and when she snowplowed to a stop at the bottom of the hill, she was laughing.

Todd's skis sprayed snow as he stopped beside her. "See? Now will you trust us with a little loan?"

"Todd!" Beth shrieked. "I knew that was what you were up to! Now stop bugging me and get lost!"

Looking discouraged, the boys shrugged and skied off toward the lodge.

A little while later Beth flopped onto the bed she shared with Alicia, exhausted. She had skied the rest of the afternoon by herself, practicing everything Marcel had taught her and varying her speed by bending her knees.

She had passed Brian, Molly, Brittany, Julie, and Sarah several times on the slopes, but none of them had paid any attention to her. They were all too caught up in their new friendship with each other to notice her.

Now Brittany was in the room getting her outfit together for dinner, choosing the perfect sweater to go with the perfect skirt, in case Marcel was there. Brian had gone to the room the boys shared, but their parents and Alicia were playing a game of Go Fish at a small table in the corner of the girls' room. There was no way she could call her friends now.

She glanced at Todd, who was sprawled on the

floor, reading a ski magazine. His cheeks were bright red from being in the wind on the upper slopes.

Beth peered over his shoulder, wondering if she could pick up some pointers.

"What are you reading about?" she asked.

"Skiing," Todd answered without looking up.

"I figured that," Beth said. "What's the article about?"

"Emergency procedures," Todd said, glancing at her. When Beth looked puzzled, he added, "It's about what to do if you're skiing on a mountain and you hurt yourself."

He turned a page, and Beth saw a picture of two crossed skis sticking up out of the snow, like the ones Marcel had put in the snow when Charles had fallen. It was a kind of SOS for injured skiers, according to the caption under the picture.

Beth made a face. "That's depressing. What other articles are in there? Anything about how to improve your technique?"

"Yeah," replied Todd. "You can read it when I'm through."

"Thanks," Beth said.

The telephone rang, and Brittany grabbed it immediately. She talked excitedly for a moment and then cupped her hand over the mouthpiece. "Is there time for tennis before dinner?"

Her mother glanced at her watch and nodded. "A couple of hours. We'll have dinner around six."

"Great!" exclaimed Brittany. "Yes," she said into the phone. "Brian and I will be there in a few minutes."

She hung up and ran to Brian's room. In a minute she was back. "We're changing for tennis," she announced, and then looked at Beth thoughtfully. "You can come, too, if you want to, Beth."

"Me?" Beth asked in surprise.

"Yeah, with you there'll be an even number of players. With only five someone would have to sit out."

Nothing like feeling welcome, thought Beth. But at least it was better than hanging out with Todd and Alicia.

After they had changed, the three of them hurried along the hall and through the corridor that connected the tennis and swimming pool bubbles with the rest of the complex. They met Julie, Molly, and Sarah halfway there.

"This is going to be great," Brittany said. "We'll play tennis with the beautiful snowcapped mountains all around us."

"It sure is—" Julie started to say. She stopped at the entrance to the swimming pool and stared. There was Marcel in his swimming trunks, heading into the pool area, a towel tossed over his shoulder.

Brittany took in a sharp breath and let it out again with a long, "Ohhhhhhh!"

Julie spun toward Brittany. "I'm suddenly in the mood for a swim. What do you say?"

"I'm with you!" said Brittany.

"What?" cried Brian. "What's with you girls, anyway? I mean, you can't seriously mean that you'd rather sit around the pool with Marcel than play tennis with me."

"Get serious, Brian," said Brittany.

Molly put her arm around Brian and put her head on his shoulder. "We'll play tennis. Just the two of us. It'll be fun."

Brian shrugged and let Molly lead him into the tennis bubble.

Okay, Beth thought. Looks like I'm swimming. I sure wasn't invited to play threesome tennis. She followed Brittany back to their room and changed into her swimsuit. By the time she was ready, Brittany had already left for the pool, so she walked back to the bubble alone.

She pushed open the door to the swimming pool bubble and stepped into the hot, steamy air. She could see Brittany, Julie, and Sarah standing at the edge of the pool, laughing loudly. Marcel was swimming laps. He couldn't possibly hear anything the girls were saying, but that didn't stop them from trying to get his attention.

"Oh, what a beautiful pool," Brittany was saying. She turned from side to side, obviously hoping Marcel would look up and see what a great figure she had.

Beth slipped quietly into the pool. She felt self-conscious that her own body wasn't that great, especially compared with the older girls'.

The pool wasn't crowded. In fact there were only three other people swimming, all older guests at Stony Lookout.

Marcel finished his laps and rested for a few minutes, hanging on to the opposite side of the pool. Of course, Brittany noticed right away.

"I'll race you girls to the end and back," she called.

"You're on!" cried Julie.

The girls took a racing stance at the edge of the pool.

"On your mark, get set, GO!" Brittany screamed.

They dove into the pool and began their race as Marcel watched.

How could Marcel possibly be interested in those girls? Beth wondered. They all act like lunatics around him.

Beth watched the race from the shallow end. Brittany was a strong swimmer, but Sarah was much faster. Julie lagged about a half-lap behind Brittany.

Sarah reached the end of the pool first and came up laughing. Brittany reached the edge next, and finally Julie.

"Wow," Brittany said to Sarah. "You're really good."

Julie laughed. "Sarah was state freestyle champ when she was fifteen."

Brittany rolled her eyes and groaned. "And you call that a fair race?" She splashed Sarah, who splashed her back. In a few seconds the three girls were all splashing each other, whooping loudly and stealing glances at Marcel.

Beth watched Marcel pull himself up on the edge of the pool and stride to the diving board at one end.

"All right, Marcel!" Brittany shouted. "Let's see if you're as good at diving as you are at skiing."

Marcel smiled and stepped up onto the board. He paused, then made his approach to the end of the board, bounced twice, and did a perfect jackknife dive. Beth was impressed. Marcel could dive, too.

The three girls went crazy, applauding and cheering his performance. Marcel swam under water and came up near Brittany.

"That was beautiful!" Brittany gushed.

"*Merci*," Marcel said, nodding to the girls. "Do you dive, mademoiselle?" he asked Sarah.

"Not really," she said, beaming at his attention.

"You swim very well," he told her.

"Thank you!" said Sarah.

"Well I'll see all of you on ze slopes tomorrow," said Marcel.

"You bet!" said Brittany. "We wouldn't miss it for anything."

"*Au revoir,*" Marcel said, and swam to the shallow end of the pool. He pushed himself up on the edge, and hopped out of the water. Then he walked toward the door, passing Beth along the way.

"See you tomorrow, Beth," he said.

"Uh, yes!" Beth answered, pleased that he knew her name. "See you tomorrow, Marcel!"

As soon as he had gone, Brittany swam toward her. She stopped a couple of inches from Beth, treading water, and glared at her. "Don't get a big head, little sister. He knew your name because of that ridiculous bit of skiing this morning. Everyone was calling your name, remember?"

Beth looked away and didn't answer.

"No one could forget someone who skis under storage sheds," Brittany remarked to the others.

"Brittany," Julie chided gently, "leave the kid alone."

"Yeah, I suppose I should leave the *kid* alone." Brittany swam a little distance away. "Come on. Let's swim some laps."

"Let's go!" shouted Julie.

Beth watched the reflection of the overhead lights

on the surface of the water. They bobbed and shimmered and bounced in the waves. She didn't care how Marcel had come to know her name. And she certainly didn't care that Brittany would laugh her head off if she knew that Beth had a secret crush on Marcel. So what if he was a lot older than she was? She could dream, couldn't she? After all, she would probably never see him again after this week. He had called her "Beth" instead of "mademoiselle," and he had said, "See you tomorrow."

Beth smiled to herself. You bet he would!

CHAPTER

8

*F*or the next couple of days the skiers in Beth's class progressed well with their lessons. Marcel showed them how to parallel ski instead of snow-plowing and moved them from the beginner slope to the intermediate. Beth was thrilled with her own improvement and felt she was beginning to look as if she knew what she was doing.

Besides that it was thrilling to be on the mountain and look down on the tiny lodge and miniature people far below.

Most days the air was chilly, but the sun was warm. She felt vibrant and alive schussing down the slope with the wind in her hair and the sound of the snow crackling under her skis. It was great, and even though she was alone most of the time, The Fabulous Five were never far from her thoughts. What were they doing? Were they having a ball at Winter Carnival? Did they miss her?

Several times she had wanted to try phoning them again. But each time, something had happened to prevent it. Once she had been called to dinner, another time Alicia had needed help with her snowsuit, and just last night Todd had walked in and seen her counting her money and had started bugging her again for money to play video games. Maybe tonight, she promised herself on the fifth day of the vacation, she would sneak off after dinner and give one of them a call.

That afternoon, after they had returned to the lifts from their lesson and lunch, Brittany said, "I know! Let's ride the lift all the way to the top of the mountain!"

"That's a good idea," said Julie. "We rode to the top last year, and you can't imagine how beautiful it is up there."

"There are lots of ski trails and different ways to come down the mountain," Sarah chimed in. "We'll pick one of the easier ones so you can handle it."

"Sounds good to me," said Brittany. "Just don't take me down The Jaws of Death."

"Don't worry," Julie assured her. "I'm not ready for a trail that's terrifying, either."

Beth gazed up at the mountain, and her heart thumped a little harder. She'd love to go all the way to the top and ski down! That would be something to tell her friends at home when they started talking about all the fun they had had at Winter Carnival.

"How hard is it to ski down?" Beth asked.

"Well, it's a lot of hard work," replied Julie. "You have to stop and catch your breath and rest your legs every so often."

"Beth, why don't you stay here?" asked Brittany. "It might be a little too hard for you."

"What are you talking about?" snapped Beth. "I can ski as well as you can."

"Come on, Beth, you've been hanging out with us constantly," Brittany complained. "Can't you find some kids your own age to ski with?"

Beth smarted at her sister's words. Brittany knew there weren't any kids her age around. Beth shot her an angry look.

"Oh, Brittany!" Sarah said. "It's okay if she comes along. She might not get another chance."

Brittany let out an exasperated breath and looked at Beth. "Oh, all right. Tag along if you have to, but don't expect me to watch out for you."

"Do you ever?" Beth said crossly.

Brittany rolled her eyes. "Come on, girls," she said to Sarah and Julie. "Let's go."

They got in line for the chair lift, which would

take them to the top of the mountain. Brittany was first, so she rode up with a man who was by himself. Julie and Sarah got on together, and Beth found herself riding with a middle-aged woman.

Brittany turned around and yelled something at Julie and Sarah. The two girls laughed and yelled back.

Beth couldn't hear a word they were saying. As usual she felt totally left out while the three of them had a great time.

When they neared the top of the mountain, Beth spotted a group of skiers maneuvering along a steep trail. One of the jackets looked familiar, and she realized it was Todd's.

"Wow," Beth whispered as she watched her brother jump over a ledge and land fifteen feet away without even slowing down. Todd really was good. He was trailing his group of friends, but he was holding his own. Beth felt a surge of pride. "Good for you," she said quietly, as she watched him thread his way through the mounds of snow called moguls.

Beth wondered if the trail he was skiing was The Jaws of Death. It certainly looked like an expert slope, but she hoped Todd wouldn't be foolish enough to try The Jaws of Death. Everyone said that it could be treacherous.

As the girls' chairs approached the lift house at the

top of the mountain, she could see skiers coming out the far side and heading off in different directions. Their colorful jackets stood out against the stark whiteness all around them.

Beth's chair moved into the building, and she inched toward the edge of her seat. A lift operator grabbed the chair and raised the safety bar from in front of her and the woman. Then Beth gently skied down the small ramp and out of the building.

"That was a fun ride," said Julie.

"Yeah," agreed Brittany, "what a view!"

"And those trails are pretty incredible," added Sarah. "But don't worry. There are plenty of easier ones."

Beth wanted to tell Brittany that she'd seen Todd skiing on one of those trails, but she was still fuming over what Brittany had said to her earlier. Instead she just gazed silently at the view below her. It was fantastic. If only her friends were here to see it with her. Beth glided down a slight incline away from the girls to a place where she could see better. There were several people nearby, some talking, some preparing to start down the mountain. Beth noticed several paths and wondered which one Julie and Sarah had meant for them to ski down.

She glanced back at Brittany and the others. They were still talking and giggling. When Brittany noticed Beth, she called, "The entrance to the trail we're taking is on your right. Go ahead. We'll catch up with you."

"Down through those trees?" Beth called back, pointing into a wooded area.

Brittany turned back to her friends and didn't bother to answer.

Beth shot a nasty look at Brittany's back. She was sick of her sister's treating her like a pesky tag-along. Who wants to wait for her anyway, thought Beth. I've been alone most of this vacation; I'll just meet up with them on the trail.

She pushed off and headed into the woods along a narrow sloping trail. She found herself on a gentle incline that let her glide along without using her poles. Beth looked up into the trees above her. There were tall pines, mostly, with a scattering of white paper birches. The deep blue sky was visible through the branches overhead. Its brilliance was startling behind the greenish-black of the pine needles.

She heard a chattering off to one side and saw two squirrels chasing each other through the branches. This is so beautiful, she thought. I *really* wish Jana and Melanie and Katie could see this. And Christie, too. I'll bet there's nothing like this in England.

Beth came to an opening in the trees that overlooked a slope and stopped above it. Turning, she looked back up the empty trail to see if Brittany,

Julie, and Sarah were coming. She couldn't see or hear them. Suddenly a suspicion entered her mind. Had Brittany sent her off in another direction so she wouldn't be following her and her friends?

"I don't know why I'm so surprised," Beth said in disgust.

Well, I can either stand here and be angry, or ski by myself and have a good time, Beth thought.

"Who cares about Brittany! Here goes," she said, sliding over the ledge she was standing on.

Beth carved a trail across the wide slope, turned and headed to the other side, making her way down the slope gradually. She felt good, and she was proud of the way she was handling her skis. If The Fabulous Five could only see me now! she thought jubilantly.

After several minutes of easy skiing, Beth could tell the slope was getting steeper. She had to fight hard to keep control, and she kept glancing ahead to see where it would get easier.

She skied down one slope, found a place to stop to catch her breath, and then took the next. She did this several times before she came to an abrupt halt on a ledge that dropped down sharply. A shiver went through Beth as she looked down a slope only an expert could take.

Oh, no, she thought. This looks like The Jaws of Death. But it couldn't be. How could she have missed the sign warning that it was an expert slope? Why had Brittany let her go this way?

A feeling of panic gripped Beth as she looked down the slope again. What was she going to do?

She looked back at the mountain. It loomed above her. There was no way she could climb all the way back up to the lift house, and there was no one else around.

"There's only one thing I can do," she whispered. "I have to ski down. But how can I without killing myself?"

Then she remembered seeing Marcel standing on a slope watching the class taking turns coming down. Every once in a while he would slide side-ways several feet down the hill to get a better position. The move had fascinated her, and she had watched carefully to see how he was doing it. His skis were pointed across the slope and his knees were bent slightly. When he wanted to stop sliding, he dug the edges of his skis into the side of the hill. With that, and the old faithful snowplow, maybe she had a chance.

Taking a deep breath, Beth let herself slide side-ways over the ridge. She slid almost twenty feet and was on the verge of panic before she was able to dig the edges of her skis into the hill and stop. All of a sudden she realized she was soaking with perspira-tion.

"So much for being cold," Beth said out loud.

Then she slipped another ten feet and stopped. Then fifteen more feet.

It was going to take her hours to get to the bottom! Beth was frightened, but there was nothing else she could do. She forced herself not to think of the danger. Instead she told herself the mountain was made of lots of little slopes and she could take them one at a time.

Beth side-slipped several more times, stopping to catch her breath and rest her legs. They were starting to quiver from the exertion.

Finally she came to an area that wasn't quite so steep. She looked above her, hoping to see skiers who could help her coming down the mountain. But no one was there. She had never felt so scared and desperate in her life.

It's all Brittany's fault, Beth thought angrily. She hasn't given me a break since we arrived at Stony Lookout. And this is the absolutely meanest thing that she has ever done. How could she send her own sister to The Jaws of Death?

Beth pushed Brittany out of her thoughts and took a deep breath. Then she snowplowed down the slope and came to another sharp drop-off. She rested for a moment, but knew she had better keep moving. The sun was starting to get low, and it wouldn't be long before it disappeared behind the mountain.

She would have to be at the bottom by then. She certainly couldn't ski this slope in the dark, and she'd freeze if she had to stay on the mountain all night.

She pushed herself gently over the edge and side-slipped downward. When she reached a resting place, her legs were aching badly, and steam from her jacket was rising in the cold air.

She allowed herself less than a minute to rest and then moved toward the next incline. Suddenly she stopped. *Had she heard something? Someone?* It had sounded like a voice.

No, now there was nothing. Maybe it had been the wind in the trees or more squirrels. Maybe she wanted so badly to see someone who might help that she had fooled herself.

But just as she was about to side-slip over the next ledge, she heard it again. Someone was calling.

"Hello!" she yelled back.

"Help," came a faint answer. "Over here."

The voice seemed to be coming from a wooded area to her right.

"Keep calling!" Beth yelled. "So I can find you!"

"Over here," came the voice again.

And that's when she spotted him sitting in the snow, leaning against a tree. It was Todd, and he looked hurt.

CHAPTER

9

"Todd!" Beth struggled to turn her skis in his direction. "Are you okay?"

As she hurried toward her brother, she realized he definitely was not okay. One of his skis was lying broken nearby, and he was gripping his ankle. His face was twisted in pain.

Todd managed a small smile. "Boy, am I glad to see you."

"What happened?" Beth asked as she released her ski bindings and knelt beside her brother.

"The other guys got way ahead of me, and I was trying to catch up. I crashed and hurt my ankle. I think it's broken."

"Let's get your ski off," Beth said.

Todd squeezed his eyes shut and moaned softly as she gently removed his remaining ski and stretched his hurt leg.

"Easy, easy," Beth said soothingly. "What made you think you could ski The Jaws of Death? You could have killed yourself."

Todd rolled his eyes. "Tell me about it." Then a confused look came over his face. "What're you doing here, Beth?"

"I took a wrong turn," she answered. "I'll tell you about it later. Now we'd better concentrate on getting you warm."

Beth unzipped her jacket and spread it out on the snow next to him. "Can you move over onto my jacket?" she asked. "I don't want you to catch cold."

"What about you?" Todd asked, scooting onto the jacket and carefully dragging his hurt ankle along.

"I'm wearing long underwear, two shirts, and a sweater," Beth answered. "Besides, I can move around to stay warm. You have to stay put."

"Thanks, Beth," he said softly.

She picked up her skis and made her way back onto the slope.

"What are you doing?" called Todd.

"I'll be right back," replied Beth. She jammed one ski in the snow in an upright position and then stuck the other in beside it. Then she forced them to cross the way Marcel had done when Charles had fallen.

"Good idea," commented Todd when Beth had returned. "There's only one problem, though. Not many people come down The Jaws of Death. Most people aren't good enough to tackle it." He paused for a moment. "Including me," he added in a small voice.

"You're a great skier, Todd," Beth said reassuringly. "But maybe you're just not quite ready for this slope."

"Yeah," Todd said. "I sure am glad you came along. I was getting scared."

Beth smiled, but didn't say anything. Todd seemed so convinced that she could help him. But deep down she wasn't sure she could even get down off the slope by herself.

She looked up at the mountain. Todd was right; hardly anyone skied this trail. There was still no one in sight, and the air was totally quiet. Except for the sound of her own breathing in the thin air, all she could hear was the wind rustling lightly through the tall pine trees. Would anyone ever find them way up here?

Beth glanced back at her brother. For the first time in hours she could feel her anger at Brittany subside a little. While Brittany had done an incredibly mean thing, it was lucky that Beth *had* gotten on The Jaws of Death. Otherwise Todd would have been up here hurt and totally alone. Deep down

Beth knew that Brittany loved her and wouldn't hurt her for anything in the world. She couldn't possibly have realized that Beth was going to take The Jaws of Death. It was my fault, too, thought Beth. I was angry and distracted, and I didn't pay any attention to where I was going.

"What will we do if no one finds us?" Todd asked, interrupting her thoughts.

Beth didn't speak for a moment. She had been wondering the same thing.

"Someone will find us," she said, trying to sound confident.

She looked up and saw that the sun was starting to touch the tip of the mountain. It would start getting dark soon. What *should* she do? Should she leave Todd here and go for help?

But what if she couldn't make it to the bottom by dark? Or what if she got lost? What if she fell and couldn't get help for either of them? The questions rushed in on her.

"Hey, Beth," Todd called. "You know what I'd like right now?"

"A blanket?" she asked.

Her brother laughed. "Yeah, that would be great. But I was thinking about some of that fried chicken the lodge makes. And mashed potatoes and gravy and hot rolls. Yum."

"Mmm," Beth agreed. "You're making my mouth water!"

"And sweet corn, and hot chocolate," he continued, grinning.

Beth covered her ears with her hands. "Stop. I'm not going to listen to you."

"And it would be nice if I could have an aspirin," Todd added, his face sobering.

"I wish I had some to give to you," replied Beth, her heart aching for her little brother. She stared at him thoughtfully.

"Maybe I could at least get us out of the wind." Especially if we have to spend the night on the mountain, she thought. Of course their parents would report them missing when they didn't show up later. And the ski patrol would search for them. But the mountain was huge, and the ski trails wound in and out of deep woods. It might be morning before anyone came near to the area they were in.

She started searching around. "There. That's a good place!" she said, pointing to a small cleared area that was protected by a cluster of trees.

At the clearing Beth dropped down on her hands and knees and began scooping out the snow in the center.

"What are you doing?" Todd called.

"You'll see," Beth called back.

When she had dug a hole in the snow big enough for her and Todd to lie in, she sat down in it. The ground was frozen hard.

She looked around. There were lots of leaves caught in the brush nearby. She began gathering bunches in her arms and tossing them into the hole.

Before long she had lined the bottom and sides of the burrow with leaves. Todd and she could lie in it and pull the rest of the leaves over themselves. It would be better than being out in the open. And they would be able to hear any members of the ski patrol who came close and see their searchlights.

Beth stood up and looked around. Was there anything else she could do to protect them from the night wind? There was one more thing.

She started gathering broken limbs from the pine trees and poking them into the ground all around the nest she had made. This would serve as a fence to block the wind. Next she yanked small clumps of brush out of the ground and packed them all around the makeshift fence. After that she threw the snow she had scooped out of the hole onto the brush.

"What are you doing?" Todd asked.

"Making a windbreak," she panted as she got back

to her feet. "I read about it once in a novel about a pioneer family going west in a wagon train. Their wagon broke down in a snowstorm in the mountains. I always thought it sounded like a neat thing to do to keep warm in the snow, but I never dreamed I'd get a chance to try it."

When she was satisfied with what she had done, she went back to Todd. "Now," she said, "we've got to move you. I'm going to drag you on my coat. Push with your good foot, but be careful of the one that's hurt."

"Okay," Todd said.

Beth grabbed the shoulders of the ski jacket Todd was lying on. "Ready?"

"Ready," he answered.

Beth tugged with all her might, and Todd pushed as best he could with his one foot. Gradually, working together, they eased him along the path and into the burrow.

Once Todd was settled on the leaves, Beth took her jacket and put it back on. "It's really getting cold," she said, shivering.

Todd silently agreed. A few minutes later he told her, "I don't think anyone is going to find us tonight."

"Sure someone will," Beth responded firmly. "It's only a matter of time."

But inside she was not at all sure. She hoped that

Brittany and her friends would realize what had happened and send someone to look for her right away. Still Beth couldn't help remembering that it would be pitch black in half an hour. And by then they would be nearly impossible to locate.

CHAPTER

10

The forest shadows disappeared as the sun sank behind the mountain, turning the daylight gray. Beth huddled closer to Todd, trying to warm him and stay warm herself.

She couldn't believe she and her brother had gotten themselves into this situation. Beth's breath came out of her nose in a wispy-white vapor. She brushed a few more leaves over her and her brother. What she wouldn't give to be sitting in front of the roaring fire in the lodge's great room at that very moment.

Suddenly she cocked her head. "Did you hear that?"

"Did I hear what?" asked Todd.

"It sounded like someone skiing!" She scrambled to a sitting position.

"I didn't—"

Beth put her hand over his mouth and listened closely. She heard it again!

Jumping to her feet, she ran to the opening. There, standing in the middle of the slope next to the crossed skis, was Marcel!

"MARCEL, WE'RE OVER HERE!" she yelled.

"Beth! Are you all right?" he called, gliding toward her.

"My brother's ankle is hurt," she answered. "He's in a lot of pain."

Marcel removed his skis and followed Beth to where Todd was lying. He frowned as he knelt and examined Todd's leg.

"*Oui*," Marcel said, resting his hand on Todd's shoulder. "You have certainly hurt your ankle, Todd. It has swollen a great deal. Are you hurt anywhere else?"

"My ankle's enough," Todd replied grimly.

Marcel nodded and stood up. He reached into his jacket and unclipped a walkie-talkie from his belt.

"Ski patrol, ski patrol, this is Goujon. Over."

A voice responded. "This is ski patrol, Marcel, we read you. What's up?"

"I have found Beth and Todd. We are on Ze Jaws of Death. Beth is fine. Ze boy has an injured ankle, possibly broken. We're approximately a third of ze way down ze hill. We'll need a stretcher. Over."

"We'll come as quickly as we can," responded the voice. "Out."

"They're on ze way," Marcel said, clipping his walkie-talkie back onto his belt.

"Did you find us by accident?" Beth asked.

"No, mademoiselle, I was looking for you," he answered, removing his backpack and taking out a blanket. He spread it over Todd and tucked it in around him. "I heard your sister talking to her friends. She and ze others couldn't find you at ze bottom. She was worried about where you were."

"Brittany worried about me?" Beth grumbled. "That's a laugh."

"*Oui*," Marcel said. "I asked her where you had started. She described where you had gone, and it sounded like Ze Jaws of Death. I couldn't believe it. Did you not see ze sign?"

Beth blushed. "No, and by the time I realized where I was, I couldn't get back to the top of the slope. I'm sure glad you found us."

"I wouldn't have, except for ze fact that you stuck your skis in ze snow. That was good thinking."

"Thanks," said Beth. "At least I did one smart thing."

"It looks as if you did several things intelligently,"

remarked Marcel, looking at the burrow and wind-break.

"Beth dug a nest for us," Todd told him. "I'm lying on a pile of leaves. It's a lot warmer than snow."

"You were clever," said Marcel. "And this shelter you made is very professional."

"Don't flatter her too much," said Todd, grinning. "If I know my sister, it's already going to her head."

Marcel laughed. "From what I know of your sister, I doubt that very seriously."

Beth smiled and felt her cheeks warm. Such a compliment was nice to hear, especially coming from Marcel.

"Hey, Beth," Todd said, looking at her and grinning.

"What?"

"I can't wait for that chicken dinner," he said.

"Me, too." She laughed.

It was completely dark when Beth heard the sounds of more skis coming down the slope. She looked up and saw the silhouettes of three orange-jacketed ski patrol men coming over the ridge above them. Two of them were dragging a rescue sled.

"We got here as quickly as we could," said one of the men as he untied a bag from the sled.

"Ze boy's in there," said Marcel, pointing to the clearing.

"I'll get the lantern, Ron," volunteered one of the men.

Working in the light of the lantern, two of the men took Todd's boot off and put a plastic splint around his ankle. While they were busy with Todd, the third man and Marcel tore down Beth's windbreak so they could pull the stretcher into the clearing and place it next to Todd. The stretcher had a rounded bottom so it would slide easily on the snow and looked as if it were made of fiberglass. Long handles stuck out in front.

"Easy now," said one of the men. "Let's slide him gently onto the stretcher."

When they had moved Todd onto the stretcher, they strapped him in tightly. Then they moved him out onto the slope.

A shiver ran through Beth as she watched the ski patrol ready themselves for the descent. What if the sled slipped out of their grasp on the mountain? Beth soon saw she didn't have anything to worry about. One man positioned himself between the handles at the front of the sled. Another took hold of ropes at the rear. Obviously it was his job to keep the stretcher from going too fast. The third ski patrol man positioned himself in front with a large battery-powered lantern to light the way for the group. They slid Todd over the ledge and began slowly working their way down the mountain.

"Ready, Beth?" asked Marcel.

"As ready as I'll ever be," she answered, gritting her teeth.

Marcel gave Beth directions and encouragement as she side-slipped and snowplowed her way down.

"Beautiful. You're doing great!" he called when she parallel-skied down a particularly difficult slope.

The ski patrol had already reached the bottom of the slope with Todd when Beth and Marcel got there. Her parents were kneeling beside Todd.

Looking at Beth, her mother cried, "Oh, kids, we've been so worried about you. We heard you had been found, but—" She broke off, choking back tears.

Beth ran to her mother and hugged her. "We're fine, Mom. Todd hurt his ankle, but he's going to be fine."

Mr. Barry squeezed Beth's shoulder while Alicia grabbed her around the waist.

"Bethy, Bethy, I was worried, too!"

The ski patrol took Todd away to the first-aid station to call a doctor. Mr. and Mrs. Barry hurried along behind.

Brian came to Beth and hugged her hard. "Glad you're back, squirt," he said, and kissed her on the forehead.

Brittany had been hanging back, watching from several steps away. Now she walked up to Beth. There were tears brimming in her eyes.

"Beth," she said, her voice choking, "I can't tell you how very, very sorry I am."

Beth grabbed her sister and hugged her. "It's okay, Brittany. It's okay."

"I didn't know The Jaws of Death was in that direction," Brittany continued, her words muffled in Beth's shoulder.

"I know you didn't," Beth answered. "I never really believed you did."

Brittany pulled away, but clung to Beth's hand. "I was so selfish," she whispered. "I mean, just because you're younger . . ."

"Yeah." Beth sighed deeply. Brittany was finally getting to the truth. "And not as *mature* as you and your friends, right?"

Brittany looked embarrassed for an instant. "Well . . . I mean . . ." she fumbled. "Gosh, Beth, you know how you feel about Todd."

Beth was baffled. "What are you talking about?"

"You hate hanging around Todd and the kids his age," Brittany said.

"That's different," Beth remarked. "Todd's so . . ." She stopped herself from saying aloud the word she had been thinking: immature. I don't believe it. Wow, she thought. I've been treating Todd just as poorly as Brittany was treating me. And I thought *I* was the only one being picked on.

Beth looked up at her sister. "I don't really like it when Todd tags along with me, or I get stuck with him. But you know what," she added around a baseball-size lump in her throat. "I'm glad the whole thing happened."

Brittany looked at her with surprise.

"If it hadn't, I never would have found Todd," Beth explained. "Maybe no one would have found him until tomorrow . . . or later."

"You have a very brave sister, Brittany," said Marcel, skiing over to them. "You should have seen how she had taken care of her brother. If I am ever lost in the woods, I would not mind having her with me."

Beth smiled up at Marcel. It was wonderful to hear him say so, but right now all she was thinking about was a hot bath. She was going to soak for an hour in steamy, hot water until she was all wrinkled and warm down to her bones. It sounded fantastic!

CHAPTER

11

"I'd like to propose a toast," Beth's father said, lifting his water glass. The rest of the family held theirs up, too, and looked expectantly at Mr. Barry. "To Beth, for her bravery, her outdoors skills, and her caring. Without those qualities, we might not have her and Todd with us tonight."

"To Beth," murmured the members of the Barry family.

Beth smiled with pleasure. She and Todd were sitting in places of honor at the ends of the dining room table. Todd had his ankle in a cast that was propped up on a chair next to him.

"Tonight's the big night," said Brittany, putting down her glass. "The fireworks start at nine, and then there's going to be a night-ski down the hill. Julie told me that everyone who skis will be carrying a flashlight, and the skiers play follow the leader down the hill. It's going to be beautiful!"

"Can I stay up and watch?" asked Alicia. "Please! Please!"

"Yes, you can watch," her mother answered, laughing. "Let's go upstairs and get your ski pants and jacket on."

Todd thumped his foot down from the chair and grabbed the crutches that were leaning against the wall. "I'll go, too. I'm supposed to meet Jason and Mike, and it's going to take me a while to get ready."

Beth watched him hobble across the room, thinking about her conversation with Brittany. "Wait a minute, Todd," she called. She jumped out of her chair and raced to him. "I'm sorry I've been so crabby about loaning you money. If you want to borrow some to play the video games with your friends later tonight, it's okay."

Todd looked surprised. "Wow! Thanks." Then he sighed and added, "Actually I'm pretty tired, so I think I'll just hit the sack after I watch the night-ski with my friends."

"Are you sure?" asked Beth. "I really would lend you a couple of dollars."

Todd thought a moment and then shook his head.

"Thanks, anyway. But there *is* something I'd like to know. Why did you change your mind?"

Beth grinned at her brother. "Oh, I guess I just discovered that you're more mature than I realized. See you later. Okay?"

Beth remembered that she had left her ski gloves at the table and went back to get them before going up to get ready for the night's activities. Her parents and Alicia had already left, and Brittany had gone to talk to Julie and Sarah. Brian was sitting there alone, finishing a piece of chocolate cake.

Molly appeared at the table just as Beth got there, too. "Brian," she said. "Let's go sit by the fire."

Brian looked up and smiled at her. "In a little while," he said.

Molly looked disappointed. "Well, don't be too long."

When Molly left, Beth turned to her brother. "Brian, why didn't you go with her? This is your last night with Molly, and . . ."

"That's okay." Brian waved his hand to dismiss it. "I'll see her later. Besides, I want to hear more about your big adventure today."

"Believe me," Beth said with a grin, "you'll get plenty of chances to hear about that. But don't give up your last chance to be with Molly because of me.

If I had met someone special, I'd want to be with him."

"Molly is really a nice girl," Brian told her, "but she's not *special* to me the way you mean."

Beth's mouth dropped open. "The way you guys have been together so much, I thought you really liked her a lot."

"She's okay," Brian said. "But I want to do other things besides be with Molly. She's always there, always hanging around."

"You don't like that?"

Brian shook his head. "Sometimes guys don't like girls who are too pushy. If I like a girl, all she has to do is be nice. You know what I mean?"

Beth thought for a minute. "Yeah, I guess so," she said. "Molly was kind of all over you."

"I liked it at first, I guess," admitted Brian, playing with a spoon. "I mean I was flattered, but after a while it got boring. Mostly I've just been trying to be nice to her until we leave."

"You aren't going to write to her, then?" asked Beth.

Brian shrugged. "I don't know. You know what a lousy writer I am." He laughed. "I hate writing themes for English."

"Don't we all?" Beth laughed, too.

"Well, I'd better go check in with her," said Brian. "I don't want to hurt her feelings. See you outside."

"You bet," Beth said. "I'm on my way up to get changed now."

After Brian left, Beth headed slowly out of the dining room, thinking about her vacation. In a way it had turned out to be exciting: the skiing lessons with Marcel, even sliding under the storage building, she thought, giggling to herself, and rescuing Todd.

I think I'll call my friends right now and tell them all about it, she thought. We have so much to talk about that I can't wait until we get home tomorrow. She pulled the small change purse out of her ski jacket pocket and headed for the pay telephone in the lobby of the lodge, thinking that she would finally get to hear about Winter Carnival, too.

"Beth, may I talk to you a minute?" Marcel called from behind her.

She stopped to let him catch up with her. "Sure."

"I wanted to tell you, again, how much I admired what you did today," Marcel said.

Beth shrugged. "Thanks, Marcel. I just did what had to be done."

"You certainly did. You are very mature." Then he smiled and added, "Just between us, you are much more mature than your sister and her friends, who are a bit silly."

"*Me?*" exclaimed Beth, incredulous. After the way Brittany and her friends had treated her all week, it was hard to believe that anyone would take her seriously. But then she thought about how Brittany and the other girls had behaved, and she knew deep down he was right.

"Another thing, you are obviously comfortable with being with all kinds of people," Marcel continued. "You take care of your little sister, and I saw you with Charles several times. I think you act much older than your age."

"Thank you, Marcel," Beth said softly. "That's the nicest thing you could have said to me."

"I must go now and get ready for ze night-ski," he said. "You will be there, won't you?"

"I wouldn't miss it," answered Beth.

Beth was humming to herself when she reached the pay phone in the lobby. She put a handful of change down beside it and slipped a quarter in the slot, punching in Jana's number. Beth hoped she wasn't calling too late. Jana and Randy might have left for the Ice Skaters' Ball already.

"Hello. Pinkerton residence."

Beth bounced on tiptoes excitedly when she heard Jana's voice and dropped more coins into the slot. "Jana, it's Beth."

"Beth?" cried Jana. "Are you home already?"

"No," Beth said. "I was dying to hear all about

Winter Carnival and wanted to talk with you. Are you and Randy going to the ball tonight?"

There was a big sigh at the other end of the line. "You mean you haven't heard?" Jana asked sadly. "Winter Carnival's a disaster. The weather turned warm and melted all the snow and ice. They had to cancel everything, including the Ice Skaters' Ball. Randy and I are just going to stay here tonight and watch a video."

Beth's mouth dropped open, and she started to giggle. "You're kidding. Then I guess I really didn't miss much, did I?"

"No way! This is the worst winter vacation there has ever been," Jana said miserably. "But, gosh! You're the lucky one. You must be having a ball!"

"I guess you could say that," replied Beth. Then she took a deep breath and began telling Jana about her adventures.

The base of the mountain was crowded with people when Beth and her family got there at nine. They found a place where they could put the folding chair the Martins had loaned them for Todd. Once he had settled in the chair, Mike and Jason joined them. They packed some snow into the shape of a footstool for Todd to rest his cast on and crouched beside him to watch the light show.

"I want up!" cried Alicia, holding her arms in the air. Mr. Barry lifted her onto his shoulders.

"There," he said. "You've got the best seat in the house."

KABOOOM!

Beth jumped as the sky was suddenly lit by brilliant fingers of light.

"Wow! Out of sight!" yelled a boy standing nearby.

"Out of sight!" echoed Alicia, pounding on her father's head.

KABOOOM! KABOOM!

"Oooooh!" cried the crowd in appreciation as red and blue lights flashed overhead.

"Cowabunga!" yelled Todd.

Fireworks exploded, first to the left and then to the right, and a pinwheel began spinning its fiery spokes not far away.

"Ooooh!" cried Beth with the crowd. It was fantastic.

Beth felt a hand on her shoulder. Looking up, she was surprised to see Marcel.

"I'd like you to come with me," he said.

Beth looked at her mother, who smiled and nodded.

Wondering what it was all about, Beth followed Marcel to the ski lift, where a group of skiers were standing and holding flashlights.

"We would like for you to lead ze night-ski," Marcel told her. "Your skis are right here, and you will need this." He handed her a flashlight.

"But I can't," cried Beth. "I'm not good enough."

"Yes, you are, mademoiselle. You *are* good enough, and I will be right behind you. Trust me. Leading ze night-ski is an honor you deserve."

Beth looked up at Marcel. The expression on his face told her he meant it.

"Okay," she said.

Beth put her skis on, and she and Marcel took the first chair and began the slow ascent up the mountain. To her relief, they got off at the first ramp instead of going all the way to the top. Maybe I can handle this, she thought.

After the other skiers had arrived, Marcel gathered them together.

"Ze object is to use only one pole and to hold your light high, following each other one by one," he explained. "Beth will be our leader. Is everyone ready?"

There was a chorus of yeses.

"Then we shall begin," he said, taking his walkie-talkie from his belt. "Goujon, to base. Over."

"This is base, Goujon," came a voice from the radio. "Go ahead."

"We are ready," said Marcel.

"Roger. Let the ceremony begin," responded the voice.

Beth could hear music start up below. She wondered what size speakers they must have for her to hear it from so far away.

"After you, Beth," said Marcel. "Take your time, there is no hurry. Actually ze slower you go, ze more like a beautiful ballet it becomes."

Beth looked down the mountain at the people standing in the lights far below. *This is just like being onstage*, she thought. I love being on the stage. I can do it! I can do it!

She pushed off, heading over the edge. Holding her flashlight high, Beth turned her knees toward the hill, and began a long, arcing curve to the right.

She shifted and started a swooping curve in the other direction. As she did, she could see the other skiers in a long line behind her. Their lights made them look like dancing fireflies.

Beth crossed the hill again. It's just like flying, she thought, as the wind brushed her hair back from her face. The music, the beautiful motion, the night air, what a wonderful ending to a vacation that was almost a disaster. She would remember this moment for the rest of her life.

Here's a preview of the Fabulous Five #31, *The Fabulous Five Together Again*, coming to your bookstore soon.

"**I** bet that's their plane!" shrieked Christie, pointing out the airport window at a big jet that was landing gracefully onto the runway. Jana, Beth, Melanie, and Katie had finally arrived in London for their spring break. Her British friends, Phoebe, Nicki, and Eleanore looked at where she was pointing.

It seemed like an eternity since Christie and her family had moved to London and she had left behind her friends in The Fabulous Five. The girls were going to stay with Christie and her parents, and she planned to keep them totally busy and show them every exciting thing that London had to offer.

She'd definitely show them the Tower of London, and Connie Farrell had promised to invite them to go horseback riding at his parents' home in the country. Melanie was going to be knocked out when she saw the Farrell's estate and the way British royalty lived. And of course they would have to shop in Soho. Beth would especially like all the funky clothes and jewelry you could find there. Christie also wanted to take them to the Montague Youth Club so they could see where she and her friends hung out.

She glanced at the three girls standing alongside her. She especially wanted The Fabulous Five to meet them. She just knew they would all like each other. The only thing that could possibly be better than having The Fabulous Five together again was to have them *and* Phoebe, Nicki, and Eleanore all together at once.

Christie grinned from ear to ear as she watched the plane taxi toward the terminal. This was going to be some vacation.

But The Fabulous Five and Christie's English friends react to each other in ways Christie never expected. The Fabulous Five also get another big surprise in The Fabulous Five #31, *The Fabulous Five Together Again*.

Do you and your friends know the answers to these trivia questions about The Fabulous Five? Quiz each other to see who knows the most Fabulous Facts!

#26 In The Fabulous Five Super #3, *Missing You*, what is the name of the horse that Christie rides in England?

#27 In book #23, *Mall Mania*, what is the name of Wakeman's new cable TV show?

#28 In book #26, *Laura's Secret*, what is the name of Laura McCall's father's girlfriend?

#29 In The Fabulous Five Super #1, *The Fabulous Five in Trouble*, what video do the girls watch at Katie's house during the sleepover?

#30 In book #5, *The Bragging War*, what is the name of the rock star whom Beth brags about?

You can find the answers to these questions, plus five more questions about Fabulous Facts, in the back of The Fabulous Five #31, *The Fabulous Five Together Again*.

Here are the answers to trivia questions #21–25, which appeared in the back of The Fabulous Five #29, *Melanie Edwards, Super Kisser.*

#21 In book #10, *Playing the Part*, Christie has a date with the boyfriend of which other member of The Fabulous Five?
Beth Barry.

#22 In book #23, *Mall Mania*, what does Shawnie Pendergast lend Beth that gets Beth in a lot of trouble?
Shawnie's credit card.

#23 In book #18, *Teen Taxi*, how does Melanie's mother embarrass her in front of her friends at school?
Mrs. Edwards starts a taxi service for kids at Wakeman Junior High.

#24 In book #25, *The Fabulous Five Minus One*, what terrible news does Christie give the others?
She tells them that she's moving to England.

#25 In book #13, *The Christmas Countdown*, what will happen if Melanie and her friends can't find homes for fifteen dogs and cats at the local animal shelter?
The animals will be put to sleep on Christmas Eve.